"Have a seat." Mac

Nerves pinging, Resa perched on the edge.

"Just tell me."

"As you know, I saw my doctor Friday." Apology was thick in Juan's voice. "He wants to do a knee replacement."

Her jaw dropped. *Please, not until after Christmas. Not now.* She couldn't deal with not having a foreman.

But she tried not to let her distress show. "We'll figure it out."

"I took the liberty of doing that for you." Juan turned to Colson. "I called Mr. Mac when I got the news."

And that had what to do with Colson?

"Colson has agreed to fill Juan's spot until his return." Mac's tone was confident. As if all her worries were taken care of.

Colson. The man whom, almost six years ago, she'd become friends with. Whom she'd fallen for.

And who had gone back to San Antonio without even saying goodbye. And married someone else. And now he'd be here for seven weeks? Her heart took a nosedive.

This could not be happening. She couldn't let it.

Shannon Taylor Vannatter is a stay-at-home mom/pastor's wife/award-winning author. She lives in a rural central-Arkansas community with a population of around one hundred, if you count a few cows. Contact her at shannonvannatter.com.

Books by Shannon Taylor Vannatter

Love Inspired

Texas Cowboys

Reuniting with the Cowboy
Winning Over the Cowboy
A Texas Holiday Reunion

Love Inspired Heartsong Presents

Rodeo Ashes
Rodeo Regrets
Rodeo Queen
Rodeo Song
Rodeo Family
Rodeo Reunion

A Texas Holiday Reunion

Shannon Taylor Vannatter

HARLEQUIN® LOVE INSPIRED®

Recycling programs for this product may not exist in your area.

LOVE INSPIRED BOOKS

ISBN-13: 978-0-373-89967-8

A Texas Holiday Reunion

Copyright © 2017 by Shannon Taylor Vannatter

www.Harlequin.com

Printed in U.S.A.

Greater love hath no man than this,
that a man lay down his life for his friends.
—*John* 15:13

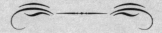

To my husband—my own personal Superman.
On top of pastoring our church,
he makes grocery-store trips, post-office runs
and endlessly chauffeurs our son.
All so I can stay home and write.

Chapter One

As her parents exchanged their wedding vows, Resa McCall dabbed at her tears.

And tried to ignore one mind-numbing cowboy, Colson Kincaid.

She and Dad had pulled it off—surprised Mom with a renewal ceremony at the Bandera, Texas, dude ranch where they'd married thirty years ago last spring.

On this first afternoon of December, the anniversary of the day they'd met, they wore replicas of their original wedding finery. The same bridesmaids and groomsmen who'd stood up for them initially now flanked her parents. Even the thirty-five-year-old ring bearer and flower girl had come. And most of their friends and family were here, too.

But try as she might, Resa couldn't keep her gaze from wandering to Colson now and then. Confident and still ridiculously handsome. Bandera rodeo hero, high school heartthrob with swoon-worthy, vivid green eyes. They'd worked together in their early twenties, six years ago. Fallen in love.

And then he'd left without so much as a goodbye. Spurred her vow to never trust another with her heart other than Jesus Christ.

"I now pronounce you still husband and wife." The pastor winked and pointed to the mistletoe overhead. "Duncan, you may kiss your wife."

Great. Resa had missed half the vows thanks to Mr. Cowboy Distraction.

Beneath the tulle-draped rafters of the great room, multicolored twinkle lights reflected off the iridescent Christmas garland as her parents laughingly kissed. Their devotion to one another was clear in their sweet embrace. As a teen, she'd longed for that kind of love. To follow in their footsteps with a committed lifetime marriage.

Until Colson Kincaid.

"Mr. and Mrs. McCall request your presence for the reception in the dining room across the foyer," the pastor announced, as a mideighties love song started up.

Her parents turned to face their guests. Wearing blissful smiles, they retraced their steps down the white-poinsettia-lined aisle toward the foyer. The wedding party followed and then Resa and her brother, before ushers began escorting guests.

Her gaze flitted to Colson, then darted away. The last person she wanted to see. Today or any other day. She'd had to invite him. How could she not, since his father was her parents' business partner? But she hadn't thought he'd actually come.

In the foyer, Mom and Dad lined up with the wedding party.

"This is so wonderful." Mom latched on to Resa's arm. The tears started up again, and before she knew it they were blubbering, with Dad pulling them in for a hug.

"It was Dad's idea."

Mom kissed his cheek. "It was perfect."

True to form, Resa's brother, Emmett, stood off to the side. Inspecting his nails, looking bored.

"Break it up, you two." Dad cleared his throat. "Greet our guests without getting them wet."

"I better go make sure everything's set in the dining room." Resa disentangled herself, dabbed under her eyes, shot a glare at Emmett.

She stepped through the doors to the reception area. "Ceremony's over." Garland lined each side of the steaming buffet, which included lasagna, zucchini and seven-layer salad. "They're greeting guests."

"All set here," a voice called from the kitchen.

There was a long row of tables in the center for her parents, family, close friends and the wedding party. Round tables filled each side for guests, graced by centerpieces with strings of imitation pearls woven through white poinsettias.

"Thanks." Resa checked her appearance in a barn-wood-framed mirror. Thankfully, her waterproof mascara had lived up to its hype.

Backing to the entryway doors, she scanned the

room. Intricate rockwork twin fireplaces bordered the space, with a wall of windows on the far end. Two massive chandeliers her father had crafted from iron wagon wheels nestled among the massive beams framing the wood ceiling.

Exactly the way it had looked in pictures of her parents' original reception. Perfect. Only better, since all the current furnishings and decor had come from her family's handcrafted log furniture store.

The door from the foyer opened. Spicy cologne filled her space. The same scent that had haunted her dreams for six years.

More like her recurring nightmare. She could feel him right behind her now. She drew in a calming breath, turned around.

Not one smart-aleck word surfaced. Probably best. Smart-aleck and Christian attitude didn't compute. So he'd finagled his way into her heart. Told her she was the only girl for him. Then left her behind, to marry someone else. It was a long time ago. She needed to get over it already.

She forced a smile as her lungs deflated. "I'm surprised you came."

"I got an invitation."

"Yes, but—"

"You haven't seen hide nor hair of me in six years." He ducked his head. "Dad strong-armed me into coming. Said it was important to your folks."

He was hatless for once. But his boots, jeans and

Western shirt proved he hadn't changed. He was still a cowboy through and through.

"This place is awesome." He pointed toward the foyer. "I did those chairs out there."

"How can you remember?" She'd designed the two cowhide wingbacks on sturdy log frames instead of the usual Queen Anne legs, but hadn't realized he'd been the crafter.

"I remember all the pieces I build. The same as you probably remember all of your designs."

She did. And those had been a challenge. When the order had been placed, she hadn't been sure she could make rustic wingbacks come together. But in the end, it worked. And the second generation owners, neighbors and friends had placed more orders, until only Rusticks Log Furnishings complemented Chasing Eden Dude Ranch.

Silence hung loud and heavy, and turned awkward. He shifted his weight.

"I'm sorry about Felicity." There, she'd said it. And she was sorry. Why was it so hard for her to say his wife's name?

His eyes dimmed. He was obviously still grieving her. "Thanks."

The doors opened. "Heads up." Devree, her wedding planner, entered the dining room. "I gave the guests a nudge in this direction, so we're about to be inundated."

"We're all set here." Resa sidestepped Colson,

but he chose the same direction and she smacked into him. It was like running into a brick wall.

"Whoa." His breath fanned her forehead.

He was still solid. Her cheeks went hot as she stepped around him and opened the door to the foyer.

Mac beamed at her. "Resa, so good to see you." Colson's dad gave her a warm hug.

"You, too, Mac. Thank you so much for doing the best man thing again."

"Wouldn't have missed it." He was such an honorable man. If only his son was as loyal.

"Please come in," she called to the guests, gesturing toward the tables. "You'll find name cards at each place setting and the ushers will help you find your seat." Her smile felt forced.

Partly because of Colson. But mostly because after the reception, Mom and Dad were leaving and would be gone until Christmas Eve. They were finally taking the time to realize their dream of a Mediterranean cruise. Leaving Resa to oversee Rusticks Log Furnishings and the family ranch.

Alone.

Her gaze landed on her brother. Fun-loving, charming ladies' man. He didn't take anything seriously and didn't have a speck of dependability in him.

Even though Mom had asked him to come home to help run things during their absence, Emmett would probably leave as soon as he took their parents to the airport. At least Resa wouldn't have to worry about keeping him in line, along with everything else.

Once the reception ended, Colson would leave, too. Then maybe her heartbeat would get back to normal and she could focus on designing furniture and keeping the ranch and the store running smoothly through the Christmas rush.

Just get through this day. Concentrate on Mom and Dad. Not Colson.

The reception got under way and Colson tried to blend in. Resa's mom was radiant as she chatted with guests at the head table.

Colson stiffened, immediately on guard when his gaze landed on Emmett sitting just down from his mom. He hadn't noticed Resa's elusive, prodigal brother. Hadn't expected him to show.

But Cheyenne was safely tucked away at the McCalls' house with his stepmom. Protected from the one man who could turn her world upside down.

With a yawn, Emmett's ice-blue eyes scanned every attractive female in the room. Nothing had changed since high school. He was still a playboy who was always in trouble, who left a string of young girls heartbroken. But he wouldn't get a chance at Cheyenne.

Emmett was the epitome of a spoiled rich kid, while Resa never gave off our-parents-are-loaded vibes. A kind, caring Christian. If only Colson had listened to her in high school when she'd tried to tell him about Jesus.

His life would have been so different.

But he wouldn't have his little girl. Cheyenne was proof that good things could come out of bad decisions.

"Can you believe Maryann asked Emmett to help me at the store while they're gone?" his dad whispered.

Colson's insides tilted. "He'll be here?"

"I sincerely doubt it. I'm surprised he even showed up for the ceremony. He'll probably leave as soon as they do."

Colson couldn't possibly stay here if Emmett did. No way around it, he'd have to let Dad down.

Seated at the head table, Resa avoided his gaze. Maybe he should have stayed in the truck. Steered clear of Emmett. And her.

But one glimpse of Resa still twisted his insides into a pretzel.

Forget-me-not blue eyes still beautiful despite the hurt he'd put there—turned icy when she looked at him. Her silken inky hair, creamy skin, delicate features always turned heads. Her lacy red dress only highlighted her beauty. Yet she'd never married. Never even dated after him, from what he'd heard through the grapevine.

After what he'd done to her, she probably thought he and all other men were just like her brother. And Colson had purposely let her think it.

His father pushed his plate away. "There was a time when I thought you might marry her."

Colson's breath caught. "Who?"

"Who." Dad chuckled. "That girl you haven't taken your eyes off of. That spring when you worked at the ranch and y'all dated, I thought it would last."

"I had to do the right thing." He'd turned his back on her. "Felicity needed me. And now that she's gone, I have to focus on Cheyenne."

"But things are different now. And Cheyenne could use a woman in her life." Dad patted his knee. "Just because your marriage wasn't good— just because your mother divorced me—it doesn't mean you shouldn't give love a chance. Look at them."

The elder McCalls exchanged a kiss. There was a lifetime of love obvious in their smiles.

But his mother hadn't only left Dad behind. She'd left Colson. Not because she'd died, but on purpose. One day, she'd thrown him the perfect birthday party. The next day, she ran off with another man. Never looked back, called, sent letters or emails. Nothing.

At the tender age of nine, he'd decided to never love another woman. And he hadn't. Not even Felicity. Until Resa McCall got to him. Took him to church. Introduced him to Jesus. And by trusting in a man he couldn't see, he'd learned to trust her. Had fallen for her.

But then his past mistakes had caught up with him. Felicity had dropped her bomb. In doing the right thing, he'd left Resa feeling abandoned, just as he'd felt when his mother had left. Trashed any chance of anything happening with the only girl he'd ever loved. Trashed her heart in the process.

Her gaze met his, then skittered away.

The longing to explain boiled in his gut. To tell her why he'd married Felicity. To share how miserable his marriage had been. To dislodge the distrust he'd embedded in Resa's eyes. To make it up to her, the only person he'd ever intentionally hurt. His time working here would be easier if he cleared the air. But if she didn't hate him anymore, his heart might end up in very dangerous territory.

He had to focus on his daughter. And even though Felicity had lied to him, made his life miserable, she hadn't deserved to die. He didn't deserve to be happy and he couldn't risk Cheyenne's biological family learning the truth.

Of all the places he needed to avoid, Bandera, Texas, was top of the list. Yet here he was. For the next three weeks until her parents returned. Maybe even the full seven weeks until the ranch foreman could come back to work. Gripping his secret and his heart with both fists.

Silverware clinked on glass as Duncan McCall stood. "I want to thank everyone for coming this weekend. A special thanks goes to our daughter, Resa, for pulling this together, all without letting her mother in on our scheme until our guests started showing up. And our gracious hosts went above and beyond to accommodate our guests and recreate our wedding day.

"Maryann and I have loved catching up with all of our friends over the weekend." Duncan raised his glass of sparkling cider. "But we've long dreamed of going on a cruise. And since our plane leaves in a few hours, I'm afraid we need to get going."

The four family members stood, did the group hug thing as the guests applauded.

"Maybe you can help Resa clean up," Dad whispered.

Something squeezed in his chest. Exactly what Colson *didn't* want to do. But he might as well get used to it. At least until Christmas Eve, she'd be stuck with him.

"When will you tell her about Juan?"

"After Maryann and Duncan leave." Dad lowered his voice even more. "If they find out, they'll cancel their cruise. I'm just glad you can stay and fill in for him. She'll have a lot on her plate."

Given a choice, she'd probably take letting one of her inexperienced hands attempt to run the ranch. Do without a foreman rather than work with him. But during this forced nearness between them, maybe keeping her ranch running smoothly would in some small measure make up for the way he'd hurt her six years ago.

Colson just needed to bide his time here, get his

head and heart together. Once this gig was over, he could go back to Kingsville. Back where nothing mattered but Cheyenne.

"None of your usual antics." Dad jabbed a finger at Emmett.

Resa loved her brother, but he was so transparent. He'd never step foot in the office or ranch during their absence.

"Who, me?" Emmett raised his hands in surrender, his playful smile oozing charm.

Bringing Emmett home to help had been Mom's idea. She hoped these three weeks would give him stability, teach him responsibility. But Resa didn't see it happening. The doubt reflected in Dad's eyes said he didn't, either.

"You're here to lend a hand. Not to flirt. Be a help to your sister, not a hindrance."

"We'll be fine." She gave each of her parents a reassuring hug. "Don't worry, have fun, and get out of here or you'll get held up at the airport and miss your flight."

"Are you certain you'll be all right? I hate for you to be alone through the Christmas rush." Mom twirled a strand of Resa's hair between her fingers. "We should have stopped taking orders months ago to cut your workload while we're gone."

"I'm fine. It's only a few weeks. Juan can handle the ranch, Mac's got the store. Emmett's here to help and y'all will be back in time for Christmas."

She tried to sound convincing, and plastered on a smile. "You've looked forward to this trip your entire marriage." She picked up a suitcase, handed it to Dad. "Now go."

"You're right." Dad kissed the top of her head. "You've got this, with or without Emmett."

"Hey." Emmett glowered. "I came when you called, didn't I? Don't I get credit for that?"

"I'll get a full report when we return." Dad frowned. "No trifling with our employees. It's against company policy."

"If you trust me so little, why did you call me?" The hurt in Emmett's tone was backed up by his wounded gaze.

But Dad didn't soften. "Here's your chance to show me what you got."

"Stop worrying." Mom clucked her tongue. "Emmett's not a kid anymore. He'll be fine." She checked her watch. "We really should be going."

Another round of hugs and Resa managed to hold the tears threatening to spill.

"Your mother made me promise not to check in," Dad whispered. "But you'll call if anything goes wrong?"

"I will. But it won't."

Mom tugged him out the door.

"You're not coming back, are you?" Resa murmured to Emmett, just loud enough for him to hear.

"Of course not. You don't need me hanging around. You got this."

True. But just once, it would be nice to be able to count on her brother.

"I'll be back for the Christmas open house this weekend, and then the night before their return." Emmett followed them out, stashed their suitcases in the trunk of his Ferrari and helped Mom into the back seat.

Standing on the porch, Resa waved until they rounded a curve on the wooded property and were out of sight.

Guests began to disperse and she thanked each one for coming.

As soon as the last one exited, she crossed the lobby to help Landry, her friend and owner of the dude ranch, clean up.

"Resa, we need to talk."

Mac.

She turned around to face him. There was Colson by his dad's side.

"It's business." Mac gestured to the paneled door by the check-in counter. "Your friend said we could use the office."

"Sure." Why include Colson? He hadn't been involved with the stores in six years. Resisting the urge to suck in a big breath, Resa crossed the foyer. Inside, Juan, the ranch foreman, waited in a nail-head wingback chair.

Mac settled on the leather sofa, with Colson flanking Juan in a matching chair.

"There you are." The slight Mexican man

straightened his left leg out in front of him. He'd always been kind and treated her with fatherly care. But today, his smile was jittery.

"What's going on?"

"Have a seat." Mac gestured to the sofa.

Nerves pinging—from Colson's presence and Juan's tone—Resa perched on the edge. Whatever it was, it wasn't good.

"Just tell me."

"As you know, I saw my doctor Friday." Apology was thick in Juan's voice. "He wants to do a knee replacement."

Her jaw dropped. Please not until after Christmas. Not now. She couldn't deal with not having a foreman. Not until Dad was here to fix it.

Stop being selfish. Focus on Juan. "Rest assured, I'll take care of anything your insurance doesn't cover."

"I appreciate that, Miss Resa. It's terrible timing. I wanted to tell you, but I knew if your folks knew, they'd cancel their trip."

And they would have. It was just like Juan to know that. To worry about it.

"You just do what you need to do. When is the surgery scheduled?" Her ranch hung on his response.

"My doctor had a cancellation, so he can get me in Thursday. Or I wait for three months."

Breath clogged in her chest. As in four days

away. "I know how much pain you've been in. I don't want you to put this off."

"I need to go on leave as of now. Doc wants me to take six weeks afterward. I'm so sorry, Miss Resa."

For a total of seven weeks, starting now. And what if the surgery wasn't a success? What then?

But she tried not to let her distress show. "We'll figure it out."

"I took the liberty of doing that for you." Juan turned to Colson. "I called Mr. Mac when I got the news."

And that had what to do with Colson?

"Colson has agreed to fill Juan's spot until your folks return. And if needed, until Juan can come back." Mac's tone was confident. As if all her worries were taken care of.

Colson. In Bandera. At her ranch. For three weeks. Maybe more. Her heart took a nosedive.

This could not be happening. She couldn't let it.

Chapter Two

Resa's mouth opened, clamped shut, opened again. "But what about your job?"

Colson was certain her anxiety came from being stuck with him for the foreseeable future.

"I'm on leave." He tried for a reassuring tone. "King's Ranch can handle my absence." But could she handle his presence?

Curiosity sparkled in her eyes, her question clear—why was he on leave? "There's no need for you to come here." The muscles in her throat worked overtime. "Don't we have a hand who can take care of things, Juan?"

"They're not ready, and we need to move fast while prices are down and invest in more cattle. I planned to make the trip to Fredericksburg next week. We need someone who knows good stock when he sees it."

"The timing is perfect, with Colson's experience as a foreman at the largest ranch in Texas for the last two years. And he's available." His dad focused on Resa, probably pondering her panic.

"Are you on medical leave?" Her gaze bounced

back to Colson's. "Because if that's the case, we can't put you to work here."

"No. Nothing like that." The horse Felicity had died riding flashed through his mind. The one he'd supposedly broken. After the incident, memories of her death had caused him to be constantly distracted and that inattention had almost cost a ranch hand his life when Colson had underestimated a longhorn. "My boss thought I needed some personal time." To get his head and heart together.

"Oh." Compassion was mirrored in the blue depths of her eyes. Clearly, she thought he was still grieving Felicity. More like wallowing in guilt.

"But where will you stay?"

"Since Mac and his wife, Annette, will be housesitting while your folks are gone—" Juan stretched his leg, as if he couldn't get comfortable "—Colson could stay with them."

Resa's eyes went wide, empathy obviously forgotten.

"I can get a room here at the dude ranch if you prefer."

"Nonsense." Juan flexed his knee. "There's plenty of room at the big house."

"Good thinking." Dad tapped his chin. "Colson can help keep an eye on the place while I'm at the store."

"But I don't need anyone to keep an eye on things," Resa fisted her hands.

"I won't bother you or disturb your space." It was the least he could do. Watch out for her.

"All right. I guess." Uncertainty hung in her words. "But once my parents return, Dad can handle the ranch while I see to the store. Can you stay and continue in the workshop until Juan's return, Mac?"

"Whatever you need me to do."

"Good." She focused on Colson. "You're only here for the next three weeks then."

"Give or take a few days." The muscle in his jaw flexed. Obviously she didn't want him here any longer than he had to be.

"I need to go help take down decorations." She stood.

His dad rose to his feet, as did Juan and Colson.

"You go home and rest that knee." Resa pointed at Juan. "Don't worry about a thing."

"Yes, Miss Resa." He bobbed his head and hobbled out of the room.

"I'm so glad you're here, Mac." Resa hugged the older man. She was so at ease with everyone—except Colson.

"If anything goes awry while your folks are gone, we'll figure it out together," his dad said.

"I'll take you up on that."

He gave Colson a warm hug next, with lots of back clapping. "You be a blessing here, son."

"I will." At least he'd try. If Resa would let him. "I'll walk out with you."

"I remember where I parked. Help Resa with cleanup." Dad exited.

Resa shot from the room as if bloodhounds tailed her.

Colson followed her to the great room. All the chairs, pillars and candles were gone. Boxes full of red roses and ribbons lined the area.

There was a steady buzz of a vacuum, which Resa manhandled from another woman, taking over the chore.

"Can you help me move the furniture back in?" A familiar-looking man gestured toward a side room.

"Sure."

"Great. Follow me." He stopped after a few paces, turned and offered his hand. "Sorry. Chase Donovan."

"As in Chasing Eden Dude Ranch. I remember you and your sister from high school. You were older than me and your sister was younger. Is she still around these parts, too?"

His mouth tipped down. "Eden died a year and a half ago."

"Sorry to hear that."

"You're Colson Kincaid, right? Your dad's a business partner of the McCalls?"

"Right. I'm filling in as ranch foreman while Juan has knee surgery."

"Nice. Need a place to stay?"

"I'm staying at the McCalls'."

The man's eyebrow lifted.

"Not with Resa. At her folks' house. My dad and stepmom are house-sitting while they're gone."

He noticed Chase visibly relax at that explanation. "You'll have to forgive me. Resa and Eden were friends, so I'm a bit protective of her. Good to know she won't be rambling around alone over there. Your dad's a stand-up guy."

"Is Emmett not staying?" Colson held his breath.

"Headed back to Dallas as we speak."

He let out a lungful of air. If Emmett had stayed, there would've been no way Colson could have.

"I'm not sure why her mom thought he'd stay. But I guess moms only see the good in their children."

Not his mom. She hadn't seen anything in him worth staying for.

Colson surveyed the feminine room stuffed with wall-to-wall furnishings. "What needs to be moved?"

"Everything frilly stays. My grandmother decorated this room. And my wife insists it stay this way. Grandpa did the rest. Everything rustic goes back into the great room."

"So which lady is your wife?"

"The strawberry blonde in the green dress is Landry."

"Did she go to our school?"

"No, but she, Eden and Resa were college friends. Not from around here. Didn't you get married?"

"To Felicity Birmingham. But she…" Guilt jabbed him in the gut, the way it always did when he was forced to talk about her.

"That's right. Sorry to hear it." Chase lifted one end of the sofa as Colson grabbed the other and backed into the great room.

Leaving Colson to ponder what Chase had heard about Felicity's death, exactly.

They deposited the bulky cowhide piece against one wall and Landry directed them on placement. Chase's smile turned sappy at his wife's nearness.

Oh, brother. How long would their bliss last?

A dozen more trips and the great room was put back together.

"Thanks for all your help." Landry flashed him a grin.

"No problem." Colson glanced at Resa. "If we're done here, I'll head to the house."

She ignored him.

"Um, I'm not sure if that's where Dad went." And Annette had mentioned taking Cheyenne out for ice cream. "I might need a key."

"Oh, of course." Resa grabbed her purse from a small closet, dug around in it and handed him the key.

Their fingers grazed. His pulse kicked up a notch. And just for a moment, he wished she'd look at him the way Landry did Chase. But Colson had ruined that possibility six years ago and he didn't need to fix it, because women couldn't be trusted.

Even if a few stuck around, it wasn't worth taking the chance. Especially with his daughter in the equation.

For the next three weeks, he had to help Resa with the ranch. Buy livestock, stay on top of upkeep and make sure everything ran smoothly. But that was all. He couldn't let himself get involved with her on a personal level. His heart was reserved for Cheyenne. And after what he'd done to Felicity, he had no right to anything more.

As the door shut behind Colson, Resa relaxed.

"Do tell." Landry was on to her.

Resa shrugged. "There's nothing to tell."

"You might as well spill." Devree sealed the last box of silk flowers with a screech from the strapping tape dispenser. "My sister won't leave you alone until you do."

"She's right." Chase pecked his wife on the cheek. "I'm off to do something manly to make up for all this wedding fluff."

"You know you love it." Landry shot him a wink.

"No. But I love you." He blew her a kiss and exited.

Maybe Landry would go all to mush and forget about Colson.

"So?"

Wishful thinking. "His dad is my parents' business partner. We went to school together. He was a year ahead of me."

"Is he the friend you mentioned once?"

Why did Landry have to have such a good memory? "We were friends once."

"More than friends?"

"I thought we were. But it turned out he wasn't who I thought he was."

"Really? He seemed so nice."

"Yeah. I thought so, too. But I learned my lesson." After he left third-degree burns on her heart.

"Hmm." Landry huffed. "I take it back. I don't like him at all. But you'll have to tell me why I don't like him someday."

"Trust me. Not everyone is destined for happily-ever-after." Devree rolled her eyes.

"Says the hardened wedding planner." Landry tsked as if there was no hope for her sister.

"I can't change the facts." Devree dragged the tape across a box of twinkle lights with another screech. "I bet out of all the weddings I've done, only a dozen couples, maybe less, are still married."

"That doesn't mean you should give up."

"It means why bother?" Resa held her hand up for a high five and Devree slapped it.

"Well, while you two spend your lonely evening bemoaning the state of happily-ever-afters, I have a wonderful husband to cuddle up to." Landry smirked.

The very thing Resa had once dreamed of. But her dream had died. A slow, painful, tormented death. And now she was stuck with Mr. Dream Killer himself.

"That's it." Landry stashed the last of the boxes in the closet.

"The ceremony was perfect and I never could have done it without you, Devree." Resa hugged Landry, then crossed the foyer. "I'll see you soon."

The waning sun greeted her as she stepped outside. She was bone tired. The chore of keeping this day secret for months, while contacting her parents' friends and relatives without letting Mom find out, had been daunting.

For the next three weeks, she'd have her hands full overseeing the store and the ranch, plus her designs. Dealing with Colson only added to her chores. If someone had told her this morning that she'd spend half her day with him and end up with him as a neighbor at home and work, she'd have laughed. And possibly cried.

Surely once Dad returned, he'd agree to cut Colson loose and let Mac stay until Juan could come back. Maybe she'd move her work to the store in the meantime.

But she'd tried that fresh out of college. The windowless office in the back of the store sapped all her creativity. While whinnies, stamping of hooves and the low murmur of ranch hands stoked her productivity.

She'd just have to pull up her big-girl boots and ignore his presence.

* * *

Most people moaned and groaned through Mondays. But Resa saw the first workday of each week as a new opportunity, filled with possibilities. Except today, she had to avoid Colson.

Nearing the barn, she darted to her office at the side door. A bright sunny morning. Nickers and whinnies, a freshly weaned calf bawling. The smells of hay and animals. No sign of the cowboy.

Tense muscles relaxed as she unlocked her office door, flipped the light switch and stashed her purse. Another flip of a switch brought to life the Christmas tree and the string of multicolored twinkle lights framing her picture window.

Blueprints for a massive cowhide-lined desk were where she'd left them on her drafting table. A desk for Colson's father-in-law. Or would that be former father-in-law now? When the order came in, she'd never imagined Colson would be here. At her ranch. She picked up her pencil, adjusted her T-square ruler and shaded along a few lines.

A new sound, like a child's giggle, interrupted her. She looked out the window. A little girl stood on the bottom rail of the fence, wearing boots and a hat almost as big as she was. Not an adult in sight. A daughter of one of the hands? Resa didn't mind employees bringing their kids to the ranch, but not leaving them alone. A child could get hurt or lost.

Resa stood, hurried for the back door, pushed it open. And nearly whacked Colson with it.

"Whoa, what's your hurry?" He stepped aside.

"That child. No one's watching her?"

"Hello?" He raised his hands, palms up.

"Oh. Well, you should stick close to her. She's so little, she could slip through the fence before you could get to her."

The little girl paid them no attention, her gaze transfixed on the mare heavy with her colt in the barn lot.

"But she won't." He crossed his arms, leaned against the barn, the sole of one booted foot planted against it like a plywood cowboy silhouette. "She's been raised on a ranch her entire five years of life. She knows that under no uncertain terms is she supposed to put one toe inside any fence."

"Who did she come here with?"

"Me. She's my daughter—Cheyenne."

Her gaze swung to his.

A mixture of emotions battled it out in his green eyes—regret maybe. Pride definitely.

Everything shifted into focus, made sense. Five years old.

That spring he came to work for her father. Almost six years ago. Realizing he wasn't as wild as he'd been in high school. Becoming friends. Inviting him to church. Watching him commit his life to Christ. Falling for him. Six weeks of sweet, fairy-tale romance.

And the next thing she knew he'd gone back to San Antonio without even saying goodbye, and married Felicity Birmingham. His on-again off-again girlfriend since high school. The one he'd told Resa he'd broken up with when he came to work at the ranch that long-ago spring. And maybe he had. But Felicity had obviously been pregnant.

With his child.

Chapter Three

Colson watched her do the math and saw the moment she realized he'd fathered a child out of wedlock. But he hadn't realized during their brief relationship that he had a pregnant ex-girlfriend waiting in the wings.

More worrisome than Resa believing he was on shaky moral ground would be if she recognized the truth in Cheyenne's eyes.

"Your folks never told you?"

"We don't really talk about you." Resa's mouth formed a tight line. "I've been much too busy to keep up with your life."

Of course. "Can you say hello, Cheyenne?" The little girl didn't budge—nor make a sound. She was back in her shell. He should have known uprooting her might be jarring.

"Shouldn't she be in school?"

"She only turned five last month, so she won't start kindergarten until next fall. Missing a few weeks of preschool before Christmas break won't hurt anything." He'd just reinforced the fact that only a matter of months after he'd romanced Resa,

Felicity had given birth to Cheyenne. A child he'd thought was his.

He saw her swallow hard. A bitter pill?

"She's a great kid. Won't be any trouble."

"My only concern is you being distracted by work and her wandering off."

Back to business. "She won't. Dad's wife agreed to babysit. Annette's really good with her." Colson's gaze went back to Cheyenne. "She's everything to me."

"I can see that." Resa turned toward the barn. "I better get back to my office."

"What time does the store open?"

"Ten. But my office is here."

"Here?" As in at her house? He hadn't seen that coming.

"In the barn." She gestured to the door she'd almost taken him out with.

"You design furniture for Rusticks—in the barn?" He'd thought it odd when he'd seen the huge picture window on the back of the wood structure.

She chuckled. "I'm not really the corporate, windowless-office type. I have a conference room at the store where I meet with clients. But I do my drafting and designing here." Her gaze went past the fence to the horses grazing in the distance, the massive expanse of clear blue sky. "The sounds of the ranch, the smells." She drew in a deep breath. "I'm inspired here."

This wasn't what he'd signed up for. The reasons

he shouldn't be here just kept stacking up. He'd expected her to be at the store from dawn to dusk. Instead, she'd be right here with a massive window on his world. On his daughter.

Lord, don't let her see what I see when I look into Cheyenne's eyes.

But did he see the evidence only because he knew the truth? He'd been clueless for several years. Maybe Resa would be, too.

He'd held on to this secret too long for it all to fall apart now.

"See ya later." She opened the barn door, stepped inside.

Would working in such close proximity stir up his old feelings for her? He'd just have to man up and make sure it didn't.

Because no matter how beautiful she was, how vulnerable or how caring, she was a woman. And women couldn't be trusted.

Not when she represented a very real and present danger for Cheyenne. And at all costs, he had to protect his daughter.

"Ready to go inside, princess?" He strode to the fence, sidled up beside her. Baby shampoo and innocence untied the knots in his insides.

"Un-uh, Daddy." Dark silky hair tumbled with a decisive shake of her head.

And hearing her call him Daddy melted him like butter.

"See how big that mare's belly is."

Huge blue eyes met his—a tinge of fear in their depths. "Is there a baby in there?"

"There sure is. She should have a foal sometime while we're here."

"I don't wanna pet it." Her chin trembled.

He scooped her up. "You don't have to. But it'll be really small, so you might change your mind."

"I won't." Her arms locked around his neck and she buried her face in his shoulder.

"It's up to you, princess." If only he could take away her fear. Take away her memories. No child should watch her father kill her mother.

The blueprints blurred and Resa's traitorous gaze bounced up to the window.

Colson was holding her now. The little girl's knees were clamped at his waist, arms tight around his shoulders, her face hidden in his neck. He had a child.

How had she not known that?

Because her parents knew how badly he'd hurt her, and his name had been off-limits since she'd learned he'd married Felicity.

She should have at least said hi to the little girl. But she'd been too shocked to think. And the child had never even looked her way, she'd just focused on the mare. So quiet and withdrawn. Was she shy, or somehow traumatized by her mother's death?

Colson kissed the top of his daughter's head and

Resa's heart did a flip. Why did a cowboy with a little girl make her go all warm and fuzzy?

Because he wasn't just *any* cowboy.

The *Bonanza* theme song started up on her cell phone. Mom.

"Hey. Are you on the boat yet?"

"About to board." She sounded happy. "All our guests got home safely?"

"I haven't heard any different."

"It was so nice seeing everyone. Everything okay there? Emmett's not giving you trouble?"

The least of her worries and long gone. "Everything's fine." *Except Juan's having surgery. Colson is here to take his place. And he has a daughter y'all never warned me about.* But if they knew any of that, they'd be on the first plane back. "Don't worry. I've got this."

"I know you do. Your father and I have complete confidence in you."

"So, stop worrying about me and have fun. I love you."

"I love you. Your father wants to say hi."

"Hey, Dad. Go have fun. And don't call me again."

His warm chuckle eased her tense shoulders. "Don't you want to know when we get on the boat?"

"Text me pictures. But don't check in. Everything's fine here. Enjoy your cruise. I love you. And goodbye."

"I love you, Miss Bossypants."

"You're the one who left me in charge." She ended the call, looked back to the window.

Deep, rich laughter. Colson held his daughter belly up, tickling her tummy. She writhed and cackled with glee. Okay, maybe she wasn't so withdrawn, after all. At least not with her father.

The realization that Cheyenne even existed was still sinking in.

Maybe tonight, Resa would fix them a meal, make a point to get to know the child and prove to Colson she really was over him.

It was suppertime, but food was the last thing on Colson's mind. He'd let Cheyenne spend an hour with him this morning to get her acclimated to their temporary home. But his day had stretched long after Annette retrieved her. His heart did triple time as he let himself in the McCalls' house, the way it always did when he'd been away from his daughter, even if only for a few hours.

Last night he'd seen that the house was much as he remembered. Large, but not as grand as the McCalls could have afforded. Massive beams, rustic design, a veritable showroom full of Rustick's furnishings. A lot like his dad's. He could hear Dad's voice, Annette's, and a child's giggle that warmed him from the inside out.

Cheyenne lay on the yellow pine floor, her dark curtain of hair framing her face, a frown of concentration there as she colored a princess's hair pink. Dad and Annette were smiling on from the nailhead log couch.

Colson plopped down beside Cheyenne.

"Daddy." She shrieked, pushed up and barreled into him.

"How's my little beauty? Do you like the new digs?"

"It's okay." But she only had eyes for him.

If he could just bottle these moments...

"Wanna color?"

"Can't wait."

She wiggled out of his arms, returned to her coloring book, pointed to the prince next to her page. "You can do him."

"What color hair should he have?" He lay flat on his belly beside her.

"Blue since he's a boy."

"Blue it is." He grabbed the crayon and went to work. He looked up when he felt his dad's and Annette's scrutiny. They were holding hands, both of them grinning at him. Married four years, they were obviously still crazy about each other. "What?"

"Adorable." Annette shot him a fond wink.

"Thanks for helping out with her."

"We had fun. I felt like a teacher again. Cheyenne will keep me in practice for subbing again next year."

Though Annette clearly loved teaching, she didn't seem to regret going from full-time to being a substitute when she'd relocated to marry his dad. At first, Colson had been leery of the new woman in Dad's life. He hadn't wanted to see his father get hurt again. And his hackles had gone up when Annette had gently suggested Cheyenne needed counseling last year.

But she'd been right. He'd watched his little girl slowly come out of her shell over the last few months. Annette had been good for Dad. Good for all of them. Colson had sympathized when he'd learned her first husband had cheated on her, left her for another woman. She'd been just as wounded as Dad, so Colson had gotten to know her. Trust her even, which was rare for him.

"I better do something about supper." Annette stood.

"You don't have to slave over us." Colson finished the prince's hair. "I'll make us sandwiches or something."

"Nonsense. Cheyenne needs more than deli meat to grow on." She headed for the kitchen.

This hiccup would be rough on all of them. New surroundings for Cheyenne. Her biological family—still in the dark—within a stone's throw. Dad and Annette uprooting their lives, sharing a house with Colson.

If his dad only knew the pickle Colson was in. But he'd let Dad down so much in the past. And Dad had never asked much of him. The least he could do was keep the McCall ranch running well during their absence. He'd just have to ignore Resa.

The doorbell rang.

"I'll get it. But it feels funny answering the Mc-Calls' door." Dad hurried to the front of the house.

Colson could hear a feminine voice. He couldn't make out the words, but he knew it was definitely Resa, making herself hard to ignore. Two sets of footfalls sounded as they made their way back to the great room.

Colson stiffened. *No, Dad, keep her away from Cheyenne.*

Maybe he should have told him the truth. But he knew his dad would want him to tell Resa. And he couldn't do that. He couldn't risk losing Cheyenne.

Colson looked up, shifted his position as his old rodeo injury flared heat through his shoulder.

"Isn't this nice." Dad held a large red pot with hot pads. "Resa brought us chicken and dumplings. And perfect timing, since Annette was just about to rustle us up a meal. I better go head her off." He continued toward the kitchen.

"I love to color." Resa shoved her hands in her pockets. Awkward, but her eyes softened as she watched Cheyenne. There was no judgment or teasing toward him, even though he currently held a crayon labeled cornflower blue.

Cheyenne's gaze never left her work; her crayon never stopped moving.

"We didn't get to meet this morning. I'm Resa." She strolled over, then settled across from Cheyenne.

She glanced up at Resa, her eyes widening because of this new adult invading her space, then focused once again on her picture.

"I really like the princess's hair pink." Resa smiled.

Seeing Cheyenne's pale blue eyes didn't seem to bring any new awareness to Resa.

Colson relaxed a bit.

"My teacher always wanted me to make it yellow, or brown, or black," his daughter murmured. "But I told her pink is for girls."

How had Resa gotten her talking? Usually Cheyenne clammed up around anyone she didn't know.

"I like the way you think."

Cheyenne glanced up at her again.

"I always wished I had purple hair." Resa tentatively reached over, twirled a strand of Cheyenne's hair around her finger.

"Really?" Cheyenne's crayon broke. "Uh-oh." She reached for another pink one. "But pink would be better."

"I agree. Maybe we can color together sometime."

"Maybe." Cheyenne's voice rose an octave. Interested? Or nervous?

Resa stood. "I'll let myself out."

The right thing to say battled in Colson's throat.

"Sure you don't wanna stay for supper, since you cooked it?"

"I appreciate the offer. But I'm good."

"Thanks for the dumplings." Relief ebbed through his stiff muscles. "My favorite."

"Yeah, I remember." She shrugged. "And most kids like them. I didn't know what Mom left in the fridge or if Annette had a chance to go shopping. So I thought I'd help y'all get settled in." She scurried for the door. "See you tomorrow."

And the next day. And the one after that. He rolled over on his back.

"Daddy, you're not finished."

"I know, princess. Just resting my shoulder." She wiggled over to him, buried her head in his chest.

He'd passed the test. Resa had seen Cheyenne up close and personal. And hadn't figured out that Emmett was his daughter's true father.

Chapter Four

Christmas lights bordered the entire storefront, casting a glow on Jed. Rustick's former furniture crafter had his head bent, intent on his work.

"Morning, Jed." Resa neared the church pew that had sat outside her family's store for as long as she could remember. The grizzled man seated there was as much of a fixture as the pew. Wood chips and curls surrounded his feet as he dug his knife into the stock of the cane, forming an intricate pattern.

He looked up from his work, gave her a wink. "Morning."

"Got that cane about finished? I may have it sold." She adjusted the blueprint tube under her arm.

"I'm working as fast as these hands will let me." They were gnarled and twisted with arthritis, but that didn't stop him.

"It's starting to get cold. You know you're always welcome in the workroom."

"It's still pleasant enough so far. Your folks' ceremony sure was nice. How's the cruise?"

"I'm worrying they may decide to never come home. They've been sending me pictures from the ship. I can't believe this is only the second day they've been gone."

"Heard about Juan." Jed nodded, never looking up from his task. "And the Kincaid boy."

"You probably remember Colson when he trained with Dad and Mac here. Before we expanded to San Antonio." Her heart did a painful thud. Why was it still hard to say his name? "I better get inside. I'm meeting with a client."

She entered the store. There was a massive tree by the door covered in rustic wooden star, cross and dove ornaments—each intricately carved by Jed long ago. Christmas lights surrounded cedar mirrors, barnwood-framed paintings and even an ash dining table.

"Morning, Nina. The decorations look nice."

"Thank you." Tall, with salt-and-pepper hair and always stylish from head to toe, Nina had been with the store since Resa's teenage years .

There were no customers yet. "Everything running smoothly here?"

"Like a well-oiled machine. Heard from your folks?"

"Having the time of their lives. Show Mrs. Birmingham to the conference room when she arrives."

"Of course."

Resa continued to the back of the store, entered

the conference room, removed the blueprints from the tube and arranged them on the long table. Nina had been here, too. A small fiber-optic tree lit a shelf in one corner of the room.

The phone at the end of the table buzzed. An in-house call.

She grabbed it. "Resa speaking."

"Colson Kincaid would like to see you." Nina's tone was all business.

But the phone almost slid from Resa's grasp. The soft, instrumental, Christian background music usually soothed her, but every nerve ending she possessed jangled.

Nina cleared her throat on the other end of the line.

"Give me a minute." Resa sucked in a quivery breath. "And then send him in." She hung up, pressed her hands on the glossy live edge cypress table. Counted to ten. Out loud.

A knock sounded at the door.

She straightened, raised her chin. "Come in."

"Sorry to bother you, but the feed store won't let me put anything on the ranch account." Hat clasped to his chest, Colson cocked an eyebrow.

Why could she never get enough air when he was around? His mere presence drained all oxygen from the room.

"I'm sorry. I failed to let them know you were on staff." She grabbed a paper clip from the corner of the table, straightening and bending it between her fingers. "I have a meeting with a client, but I'll make the call as soon as we're finished."

"I thought maybe you'd decided to work here to avoid me." He sank into one of the chairs at the long table, ignoring her subtle hint for him to go.

She swallowed hard. No. She wouldn't fall under his spell. It had been six years since he'd broken her heart. And she hadn't missed him. Not one iota.

Even though she understood why he'd left her, he should have been man enough to tell her the truth instead of pulling a disappearing act.

"I'm not hiding." Her mouth went taut and she gestured to the blueprints. "I'm meeting with your mother-in-law, actually." Or was it former mother-in-law, since Felicity's death?

"Hyacinth is coming here?" He jumped up, clamped his hat on his head.

"Any minute. I was shocked when she placed the order. Her first one with us. Always struck me as the Queen Anne type, but apparently her husband bought a cabin."

"I have to get out of here." He strode to the door.

The phone buzzed. "That's probably her." Did they not get along?

"I haven't told her we're here yet." Colson scanned the room as if looking for a place to bust through the wall. "It's complicated—I wanted to get Cheyenne settled first."

"I'll hold her off if you want to slip out the back." Resa picked up the phone. "Yes, Nina."

"Mrs. Birmingham is here."

"Give me a few minutes." She hung up, gestured to the back of the building. "Turn right in the hall."

"Thanks." He opened the door.

"Colson?" Hyacinth Birmingham said from a distance.

But not for long. Colson backed into the conference room as his mother-in-law approached.

Hyacinth stalked inside, her nose in the air. "I didn't know you were in town."

Nina was right on her heels.

"Thank you for showing Mrs. Birmingham in," Resa told her. More like blasted her way in.

Nina splayed her hands, stepped out and shut the door.

"Is Cheyenne with you?" The woman, a San Antonio blue blood, was positively irate.

And Resa wanted to bolt for the door herself.

"I was going to call you." Colson's tone attempted to soothe.

"How long will you be here? When can we see Cheyenne?"

"I'm the foreman at Resa's ranch until Christmas Eve. We'll set something up soon."

Hyacinth's fists clenched. "Almost all month. Why haven't you called us?"

Oh dear. "Colson just arrived Sunday and it was all very last-minute," Resa interjected. "I'm certain he'd love for you to see your granddaughter."

Why was she defending him? Because she didn't

need this kind of drama in her store? Because she'd seen the evidence that he was a good father?

Both. But also probably because it was happening all over again—she was being drawn to him.

"Who's watching her while you're at work? What about school?"

"She's with Annette and they're staying brushed up on her preschooling, so she'll be ready for kindergarten next year."

"Of course." Hyacinth looked toward the ceiling. "A woman she's no blood relation to."

Colson's jaw tensed; his eyes turned steely. "Are you offering to preschool her?" His voice dripped with sarcasm.

If only Resa could melt through the floor.

"Of course not. But she could stay with us. We keep a nanny on staff."

"Absolutely not." He swallowed hard. "I like having her near and she loves Annette, who's actually a teacher."

"Just wait until Nigel hears about this." Hyacinth propped her hands on her hips. "I can't believe you plan to keep Cheyenne away from us. How dare you—after you killed our daughter."

Resa swung her gaze to Colson.

All color drained from his face.

"It's not like that, Hyacinth. I can assure you." Colson clenched his teeth. "I was just trying to get Cheyenne settled in. You know it's hard for her to adjust to change." *And she's scared of you.* Actually, truth be told, he was, too.

"Well, having her grandparents near would lessen the change." Her nose went higher in the air. Still snooty.

"Mimi. Let's go already." Hyacinth's other granddaughter, Jasmine, now nine or so, flounced into the conference room. Hands on hips, tapping her Gucci-clad foot, she was the spitting image of her mother—Felicity's sister, Lucinda—in looks and attitude.

"I'm sorry." Nina rushed in. "She got away from me."

"Jasmine." Hyacinth glared at Nina. "I told you to stay with the nice lady."

"It's okay, Nina. Babysitting isn't in your job description." Resa smiled at her flustered employee, then turned to her customer. "I'm sorry, but my floor manager has work to do."

Hyacinth tugged at the hem of her thousand-dollar jacket. "I didn't have any choice other than to bring her. The nanny just up and quit. With no notice."

Colson had a pretty good idea why. He slipped his phone from his pocket. "Jasmine can play a game on my cell while you and Resa talk furniture."

"Puhlease. I've got my own phone." The little girl crossed her arms and perched on the edge of the sofa, as if she didn't plan to stay long.

He couldn't risk alienating a wealthy client like Hyacinth by giving her rude grandchild a tongue-lashing. If she left the store unhappy, half of Texas would hear about it. Besides, he needed to stay in her good graces. Make her irate enough and she just might try to take Cheyenne from him. Especially if the truth got out.

"I'm excited about your desk and I'm glad you're here." Resa pulled out a chair. "I've got some ideas I wanted to run by you."

"Maybe I should come back once I get a new nanny. Come along, Jasmine." Hyacinth patted her immovable hair, tucked in a perfect chignon at the base of her neck. He'd made the mistake of calling it a bun once.

The little girl spewed out an exasperated sigh and flounced to the door.

"Call me, Colson." Hyacinth pursed her lips. "We'll expect a visit tonight."

"Aren't you taking Cheyenne to the Trail of Lights tonight?" Resa asked.

Huh? Was she giving him a reprieve?

"I was so busy with my parents' renewal service, we missed the parade," she added. "But the lights are on until New Year's. Why don't you join us, Hyacinth?"

Did she just throw him under the tractor?

"Oh, I don't know." His mother-in-law pinched the high-dollar fabric of her skirt. "Nigel and I don't usually bother."

"I'll arrange a hayride for us. Bring Jasmine along."

"Excuse me." The girl rolled her eyes. "I'm too old for baby stuff."

"Well, I'm not." Resa shot the child a wink. "We'll see you there, Hyacinth?"

The older woman's mouth opened, closed, opened again.

At a loss for words. Something he'd never seen. He needed to take lessons from Resa on how to handle her.

"I'm bored, Mimi," Jasmine whined.

"All right." Hyacinth took her by the hand. "I guess we'll see you tonight."

"You can't make me go," the girl wailed as Hyacinth ushered her out.

When the door shut behind them, Colson blew out a big breath. "That's why I haven't called them. I don't want Hyacinth turning Cheyenne into a snooty copy of herself."

Or discovering the truth. "Felicity had her faults, but she was nothing like the other women in her family. They've seen Cheyenne exactly three times, and Hyacinth only clamored for more because she had an audience today. Cheyenne's afraid of her." A bitter laugh escaped him. "I kind of am, too."

"Me, too." Resa giggled. "But I don't mind taking her money."

Colson squeezed his eyes closed, tried to block out the image. "I didn't kill Felicity."

"I know."

"You do?"

"You'd be in jail if you did."

"She was taking a horse I'd recently broken for a ride. We had an argument and she took off. The horse threw her." Clear as the day it happened he could still see Felicity lying there, her neck at an odd angle. "I should have known the horse wasn't safe."

"You couldn't have known. Horses are unpredictable. Not even you can read their minds."

"I shouldn't have argued with her. Not with her on the horse. I probably agitated him."

Resa's slim hand touched his arm. "It's not your fault."

He met her gaze. Her hand fell away. His guilt didn't budge.

"Why did you give me the perfect excuse to avoid Hyacinth tonight and then insist she come along?"

"If you don't arrange for Cheyenne to spend time with her, the woman might get ugly about it."

True enough. She might take him to court. Which might lead to DNA testing. Which would prove he had no claim on Cheyenne.

"This way, your daughter will enjoy herself, even though Hyacinth will be there. I figured it was better than a one-on-one situation."

"I guess you're right."

"So are you and Cheyenne coming?"

"We're in." It went against all his plans of keeping Cheyenne away from her biological family. But Resa obviously hadn't caught on—even though Cheyenne was a miniature version of her. "We'll meet you there."

"See you around seven?"

"We'll be there."

"In the meantime, don't you have a ranch to run?"

"The feed store."

"Oh yes. Sorry." Resa rolled up the blueprints, stashed them in a cardboard tube and tucked it under her arm. "I'm done here, so let's just go there."

He followed her out. He had to keep the Birminghams happy. And clueless. His gut did a sick twist. If they somehow learned the truth, Hyacinth would stop at nothing to get custody of Cheyenne. To let a nanny raise her. To add the child to her possessions.

Over his dead body.

But Resa couldn't learn the truth, either. A delicate tightrope stretched taut underneath him. And the wire kept shifting under his feet.

Despite Colson, his dad and Annette surrounding her, Cheyenne had gone silent and withdrawn when she'd seen Hyacinth.

Resa absorbed all Colson's tension. Cheyenne's discomfort was her fault.

Hyacinth reluctantly sat on a hay bale and paid

more attention to the damage the straws supposedly made in her pricey pantsuit than to her granddaughter. Jasmine had pulled a no-show. Probably a good thing. Resa's friends Landry and Chase, along with his parents, made up the rest of the crew. Putting some space between Resa and Colson.

The ranch truck pulling the wagon rounded the corner and they got the first glimpse of the lights. Cheyenne audibly gasped and seemed to forget all about her grandmother.

Nigel Birmingham, just as down-to-earth as his wife was snooty, focused completely on his granddaughter. "There's a cowboy boot bigger than would fit any cowboy I've ever known." He was clearly intent on soothing her with his heartwarming, silly running commentary on each display.

The little girl giggled, obviously at ease with her grandfather.

"Except Big Tex. You ever been to the State Fair of Texas?"

Cheyenne's eyes widened. "Daddy took me this year. Big Tex is really big and I was scared of him cause he talks. But Daddy says he's just a big old statue with a recorded voice and they take him apart and put him in a truck once the fair is over."

"I think somebody stole Big Tex's boot. What do you think?"

She giggled again.

"Which one's yours, Resa?" Nigel asked.

"The nativity."

"Ah." He grinned. "It's nice."

"Do you have one?"

The wagon hit a pothole, jostling them a bit.

"The angels overlooking the nativity."

"We have a display?" Hyacinth whipped around to face her husband.

"For years. It doesn't cost much. You can't have a nativity without angels, and it makes people happy. You can't put a price on that, dear."

"You helped put up the lights, Poppy?" Cheyenne moved a bit closer.

"Nope. I just pay to have the angels put up every year. But there are lots of Christmas festivities to come. We could get in on Singing in the Saddle in a few weeks."

"Really, Nigel, don't encourage her." Hyacinth scoffed.

"What's Singing in the Saddle?" Cheyenne, her face aglow from the lights surrounding them, ignored her grandmother.

"It's a trail ride of sorts with caroling. People ride horses or wagons around Bandera."

"But I don't want to ride a horse."

"How about a wagon?" Resa patted the hay bale where she sat. "You can ride in this very wagon."

"Can we go, Daddy? Can we?"

"We'll see."

"It wouldn't be Christmas caroling without you." Nigel sent Colson a hopeful smile. "But just in case, we can sing now." Nigel started "Silent Night" off, his deep rich baritone echoing through the crisp air.

As voices joined, Landry elbowed Resa. "So why is the cowboy still here?"

Resa whispered the explanation.

"Why didn't you tell me?"

"Because it's no big deal."

"And the little girl is his?"

"He was married. But his wife died two years ago."

"Hmm."

"There's no 'hmm.'"

"So why did you invite him on the hayride if you don't like him?"

"I invited Cheyenne on the hayride." She whispered the whole thing about Hyacinth demanding a visit.

"And you care about this child because?"

"I don't know." Resa shrugged. "She's just a little girl. Who lost her mother. And now she's had to move away from everything she's ever known because of me. The least I can do is ease her discomfort with Christmas lights."

"Hmm."

"You already said that. It's temporary. They'll only be here until my parents get back. And then they'll move back to Kingsville."

So why did that thought make her feel sad and lonely?

Chapter Five

Colson pulled into the lit church parking lot and parked.

"Do we have to go here, Daddy?" The insecure little voice from the back seat tugged at his insides.

"God wants us to gather for worship and fellowship." And maybe there would be kids her age to make friends with and help with her transition.

"I know. But it's big and scary."

"Church isn't scary. You may not know the people here, but church folks are usually nice. Grandpa Mac and Nette will be here." He closed his eyes. "And Resa."

"Really?"

"Yep."

"Okay."

He got out, opened the back door and helped her down from her car seat, which she'd already unfastened. Hand in hand, they crossed the parking lot and slipped inside. Several people greeted them and he immediately felt welcomed, just as when he'd attended six years before. But none of the greeters had any children with them. And as each person spoke to them, Cheyenne withdrew more.

Resa was already here, flanked by Landry and Chase on one side, Annette and his dad on the other. She looked up when he took his seat beside Dad. Colson flashed her a smile. She waved as he settled Cheyenne in his lap. Thankfully, the pianist started up and the song director called out a page number.

The stained glass windows splashed multicolored prisms on the walls. Not much had changed. The hundred-year-old church was like a time capsule. If only it could comfort Cheyenne the way it did him.

Three songs later, all the kids and a few adults got up and headed for the back of the sanctuary. Except Cheyenne. Apparently they had classes on Wednesday night, but he knew she'd never go.

A kind-eyed lady stopped at their pew. "I'm Marilyn Whitlow."

"I'm Colson Kincaid and this is Cheyenne." Little arms wrapped around his neck.

"What a pretty name. You look just about the age to come to my class. We'll read a story about Jesus, maybe do some coloring and sing some songs. Would you like to join us?"

Cheyenne buried her face in his chest.

"Maybe next time."

"Of course." Marilyn turned away.

"Is she gone?" The muffled question was warm against his heart.

"Yes. But she seemed really nice and you love to color. Wouldn't you rather go have fun with kids than stay here with me?"

"Don't make me go."

"It's okay. You can stay with me." He rubbed her back.

"Can I sit in Resa's lap?"

The breath went out of his lungs. "I'm not sure she's up for that." He sure wasn't.

"Please."

He leaned forward, looked around Dad and Annette.

Resa noticed him.

She wants to sit with you, he mouthed.

A smile took over her entire face and she nodded.

"She said yes."

Cheyenne pulled away from him, taking a piece of his heart with her. She clambered down, over Dad's and Annette's feet, and Resa helped his child into her lap.

He didn't breathe after that. And didn't hear any of the lesson.

With Cheyenne so enamored with Resa, how would he resist her?

And more than that, how would he keep his secret?

Cheyenne's slight weight got heavier as she drifted off. Resa could get way too attached. Especially since the shy little girl seemed drawn to her.

Deep down, she was glad Colson had come to Bible study this evening. She just wished he'd chosen another church. She wasn't ready to forgive him.

She was stuck working with him until Christmas. Forced to count on him to keep her ranch running smoothly. But none of that trumped that he'd once broken her heart. And even though she understood his reasons now, she couldn't allow herself to let her guard down around him. He wasn't here to stay this time, either.

Colson. In her parents' house. In her office. In her store. And now in her church. How had her life come to this?

Amens echoed around her and she raised her head. She hadn't heard a word of the closing prayer. Or the study, for that matter. Why was he so…distracting?

"Let me take her." He scooped Cheyenne out of her arms.

The brush of his fingers against her arm sent goose bumps over her.

Burden lifted, she stood and made her way to the aisle, as a hand clamped on her shoulder from behind.

"Resa."

"Evening, Jed." She turned and gave him a quick hug over the pew. "Remember to bring your wares soon. Open house is this weekend."

"I appreciate you including me."

"Are you kidding? Your stuff brings customers in."

"Glad to hear it. Say, reckon you could come on over tonight? I've got two walking canes, three table lamps and half a dozen candlesticks. It would be easier on me if I didn't have to load it all."

"Of course. I didn't even think about that."

"Maybe the Kincaid boy could help," Marilyn suggested. "Might get his little girl comfortable with me. Enough for her to come to my class next week."

"I knew I married you for more than your beauty." Jed winked at his wife.

"Colson," Marilyn called as he neared the exit. "Could you help us out?"

"Sure." He strolled toward them with Cheyenne still sleeping on his shoulder.

"Oh, I didn't realize she was asleep. Never mind." Marilyn stroked the little girl's hair.

"I was just trying to wake her." Colson's narrowed gaze settled on Resa. "I don't usually let her sleep through church. And if she naps this late, she won't go to bed."

And she was supposed to know that? "You remember Jed, don't you? He probably visited the Bandera store back when you were training with your dad."

"It's been a while." Colson clasped the hand Jed offered.

"I've got some carved items ready for delivery

to Resa's store." Jed clapped him on the back. "We were wondering if you could follow us to the house and load up."

"And I was hoping to get to know this little darling." Marilyn smoothed her hand down the sleeping child's back.

"I'd be happy to help."

Oh no. Oh no. Oh no. "Thank you, Colson. It's settled then—you can follow Jed there." And Resa would go straight home.

"But Jed has something he needs to show you." Marilyn clasped her elbow.

"Now, Marilyn, I told you they're not ready."

"Oh, pooh." Marilyn waved her husband's protests aside with her hand. "I don't know how they could get any more ready."

"You've got something new?" Resa's insides warmed. She'd known Jed since she was a kid. And had mourned with him when arthritis threatened his work.

"Wait till you see them." Marilyn's smile broadened. "He always second-guesses himself, but I'm trying to talk him into going on a bigger scale with these."

"She don't need to see. They're not ready."

"Please, Jed." Resa's voice blended with his wife's.

"Aw, shucks." He turned crimson. "I reckon. But if you don't think they're up to par, just say the word. Nothing amateur is going under the Rusticks name."

"Oh, good." Marilyn clapped her hands. "I've got a dessert I've been dying to thaw. That Mrs. Edwards sure can turn out a mean turtle pie."

"I'm in." Colson let out a low whistle.

"Y'all could ride together?" Jed suggested.

"No." The protest ripped from Resa. "I mean— we'd just have to come back here and get my car. It's easier if we both drive."

"All righty then."

She wanted to see Jed's newest creation. Wanted to encourage his one-of-a-kind craftsmanship. But it was bad enough that Colson was coming, too. Bad enough that she had to share pie with him. No way would she share a ride with him, as well.

"How about we go see the chickens." Marilyn offered her hand.

Though her eyes filled with wonder, Cheyenne clenched Colson's fingers tighter.

"They can't get out. They're all safe in the coop," he prompted. "I'll be right here in Jed's workshop."

Her grip loosened, let go, then latched on to Marilyn.

Maybe the kind women of small-town Bandera were just what Cheyenne needed. Even though this broadening of her horizons was good for her, letting her go was hard on him. He refocused.

Smooth wood, perfect gloss, no imperfections.

Colson opened the lid of the box. Black velvet-lined compartments. The smell of cedar filled the workshop.

"This doohickey comes out." Jed lifted the top tray to reveal more compartments. "And there's a card with my number, so they can order a silver plate with their name engraved on it."

"For an extra charge?" Resa inspected the card.

"Nope. If they buy the box the engraving is free. I figure they'll have to come back to the store to pick up the plate and maybe they'll buy something else." Jed carefully set the tray back in place. "Tell it to me straight. No two-steppin' around it."

"They're beautiful." Resa's voice was filled with awe and appreciation.

"You think?" Pride warmed Jed's smile.

"As beautiful as the one you gave me for graduation."

"Wait, you've made these before?" Colson set the cedar jewelry box down among the others. "Do we carry them in the store?"

"It's been a long time since I made any. Did one as a gift a few years back. Gave me a hankering to make some more."

"The one you gave to Landry." Resa's eyes glistened. "I saw it. Such a sweet gesture and it meant the world to her."

"She's obviously biased." Jed rubbed the back of his neck. "You sure they're good enough quality, Colson? You're not just trying to make an old man feel good?"

"You *should* feel good about these, Jed."

"Can we show them at our open house?" Resa propped her hands in a steeple, a visual plea.

Jed inspected the row of boxes on the shelf in his workshop. "If you're sure they're ready."

"They're ready. I'd stake the reputation of Rusticks on them."

"I reckon you're doing that."

She stood on tiptoe, kissed his grizzled cheek, which quickly turned scarlet.

"Let's go have some pie." Jed gestured them to the door.

"Where's the chicken coop?" Colson trailed Resa as Jed turned the light off. Eager to retrieve his daughter, he stepped outside, searched the yard by the glow of Christmas lights lining the house. No sign of them.

"Looks like they already went inside."

Cheyenne never warmed to anyone that fast.

Five strides and they stepped into the cozy kitchen, where Cheyenne sat beside Marilyn at a farmhouse table with log legs. Five saucers, each bearing a generous slice of pie, waited. A Christmas tree with multicolored blinking lights, decorated with small American Flags and ornaments in red, white and blue, captured Cheyenne's attention almost more than the pie.

"I don't think I want any pie made from turtles, Daddy." She scrunched her nose.

"That's just what they call it, darling." Marilyn patted the small head. "It's really made from yummy stuff."

"I think you'll really like it." Colson settled on her other side.

Everyone placed their drink orders and Resa helped Marilyn serve.

Chocolate, caramel and whipped cream melted on his tongue, complemented by the crunch of pecans. The only thing better than the pie was seeing Cheyenne blossom. And having Resa seated beside him. Still clueless about his daughter's parentage.

Cheyenne spooned a minuscule bite into her mouth and her eyes rounded. "You're right, Ms. Marilyn, it is yummy."

"I'm glad you like it. This is nice." Marilyn sipped her coffee. "Having young folks around. Since our kids got grown and moved to the city, it's just us old folks milling about most of the time."

"They remind me of us, when we were dating." Jed shot Resa a wink.

"We're not dating." Her voice quivered.

"You will be." Jed set his cup down. "I can spot it. Called it with Landry and Chase. When I been knowing a young'un for so long, I can tell."

"Stop it, Jed." Marilyn rolled her eyes. "You're making her turn the color of those plums."

Colson resisted the urge to see how purple looked on her. Partly because his face felt just as warm.

"What's dating?" Cheyenne popped another bite of pie in her mouth.

"I'll explain later." Colson focused on Jed. "How long have y'all known each other?"

"I was friends with her granddad. Knew yours, too." Jed shot her a wink. "Known her since she was born."

"Jed was the main crafter here at the Bandera store." Resa scooped another bite of pie on her fork. "Before your dad."

"Until the arthritis hit. I couldn't keep up after that."

"But Resa and her dad encouraged Jed to do what he could, keep crafting at his own pace." Marilyn's gaze, full of love and respect, rested on her husband. "They've sold a lot of Jed's work through the years. And won't even take a commission."

Resa stayed focused on the table. "Jed put his hours in for us. Sold a lot of furniture for us. Just returning the favor."

"I'm trying to talk him into building hope chests again."

Resa's gaze bounced up to Jed, her excited smile lighting a sparkle in her blue eyes. "You have to do it. I never got one."

"I'll make you a deal, young'un." Jed shot her another wink. "You get married and I'll make you one." His scrutiny shifted to Colson.

Colson shoved the last bite of pie in his mouth, took a swig of coffee. "It's getting late. We best be on our way."

"Look what you've done with all your teasing, Jed." Marilyn clucked her tongue. "You've run them off."

Running scared. The last thing Colson needed to ponder on was marrying Resa. Because even though he didn't trust women, and had vowed to never remarry, after a mere four days Resa was starting to look good to him all over again. In a permanent sort of way.

She pushed her plate away. "It's probably getting close to Cheyenne's bedtime and I've got an early morning trip to San Antonio tomorrow."

"Do we have to go, Daddy?" Cheyenne yawned, despite sleeping through church.

"You can come back anytime." Marilyn patted her hand.

But not with Resa. From now on Colson had to avoid her at all costs. Only work-related contact. Period. And unfortunately, there would be a lot of that over the next three weeks.

"Thanks for the pie, Marilyn." Colson stood, pulled out Cheyenne's chair and took her tiny hand in his.

"Maybe I'll see you in my class next week." Marilyn patted the little girl's shoulder.

"Maybe." Cheyenne blushed.

Resa hugged their hosts and Colson opened the door for her.

Thousands of stars and an almost full moon lit the sky as they stepped outside.

"What time is Juan's surgery?"

Her eyes widened. "Eight. You remembered."

"The reason I'm here." How could he not remember? He'd come prepared to stay until Juan's return. If her dad didn't let him off the hook, his six-week calendar officially started ticking tomorrow. "I met a breeder from San Antonio at the sale barn yesterday. I have an appointment with him tomorrow to check out a bull, so I thought I'd see about Juan while I was there."

"I get to go, too." Cheyenne yawned again. "You should ride with us, Resa."

"Oh. I don't know."

So much for avoiding her. "I guess it really doesn't make much sense for both of us to make the drive. We could drop you at the hospital, then go meet the breeder, check on Juan, pick you up and head home."

"But I want to stay until he's out of surgery."

"Not a problem. Cheyenne is always up for killing time at the zoo."

"Please, Resa."

He watched the softening of her eyes as Cheyenne melted her resistance.

"Okay. I guess I'll see y'all in the morning."

"Six thirty-ish? In case traffic is bad."

"Sounds like a plan." She got in her vehicle as he settled Cheyenne in her car seat in the back of his truck.

By the time he got on the road, she was asleep.

An hour's drive with Resa in the morning. And another back home. At least he wouldn't be hanging out at the hospital with her all day. He needed to figure out a way to teach Cheyenne not to invite her along in the future. Even though he'd taught her to be kind. He still had three weeks of navigating around Resa. And the time couldn't pass fast enough.

How had he ended up at the zoo with Cheyenne—and Resa?

"I can't believe they haven't gotten Juan into surgery yet." She checked her watch again. "It's almost ten."

"Must have been a serious emergency for the hospital to get off schedule so badly. I can take you back. You didn't have to come with us."

"Yes, I most certainly did." She smiled down at Cheyenne between them, her hands in each of theirs, fascinated by the alligators and crocodiles. "She asked me. But what about the bull?"

"If I buy him, I have no desire to keep a bull kicking around in the trailer for any longer than I have to. I told Mr. Mendez I'd call him once Juan went into surgery. That way, by the time he gets out, I'll be back to get you. Bull or no bull."

"Look, Daddy." Cheyenne tugged on his hand, her gaze fixed on the carousel.

Hmm. Maybe this could be the first step in getting her over her fear of horses. "You wanna ride?"

Cheyenne bobbed her head, her eyes never leaving the merry-go-round. "Will you ride with us, Resa?"

"Of course I will, sweet pea."

They strode to the short line. As they waited for the ride to stop, Colson inspected each shiny animal. The carousel slowly spun, the animals melodiously gliding up and down as if following a musical scale. A hippo, a tiger, but no horses. Great. Cheyenne wanted to ride a carousel and this one had no horses. Maybe a zebra would do the trick. Oh wait, there it was—a horse.

The merry-go-round slowed; animals stopped their rhythmic rise and fall. Attendants helped children down and off, then took tickets and opened the gate.

"Do you want to ride an elephant, or an eagle, or a deer?" Resa helped Cheyenne up onto the platform. "So many choices."

"How about a horse?" Colson tried for casual.

"A horse?" Resa laughed up at him. "Typical cowboy. You can ride a horse on any old carousel. At least make it a zebra."

She had no clue. No idea what Cheyenne had been through. No concept of the hours of therapy.

Cheyenne stopped, stared at the brown-and-white-painted horse. "I want to ride that."

Please don't try to talk her out of it.

"A horse it is, then." Resa helped her up into the molded saddle.

"I want Resa on one side and Daddy on the other." Cheyenne gripped the pole.

"All children, pick your animal, please." The attendant boosted another child up onto a polar bear.

Once they were all seated and holding poles, the carousel started up.

And Cheyenne giggled. "I feel like I'm flying."

"That's how I feel when I ride a real horse." Resa stayed glued to Cheyenne's side, her hands just above the child's on the pole. "Have you ever ridden a horse?"

"No." Cheyenne withdrew inside herself. The light dimmed in her eyes.

He should have explained to Resa, so she wouldn't ask questions.

"I want off, Daddy."

"You can't get off right now, princess. Just calm down. You're safe. I'll keep you safe."

"And if we ask the carousel operator to stop it, all these other kids will be sad." Resa patted her back.

Cheyenne nodded, clinging to her pole as Colson prayed for the carousel to stop. To end Cheyenne's torment.

After what seemed like at last fifteen minutes, the ride slowed, the horse stopped.

As soon as it was still, Cheyenne practically bailed off into his arms, clung to him. "I rode a horse, Daddy."

"I'm so proud of you."

"It was kind of scary. But it was fun for a little bit."

The *Bonanza* theme started up. Resa dug her phone from her pocket. "Hello?... Finally. I'll be there soon." She hung up.

"Juan's surgery?"

"They just took him back. I'm sorry to cut your zoo visit short, Cheyenne. Maybe we can come again sometime."

"It's okay. I saw all the animals and I rode a horse on a carousel." Cheyenne said it as if it was at the top of her bucket list.

"You did great, princess."

He swung her down to the ground and they exited the gate. Cheyenne had gotten scared when Resa mentioned real horses, but with his daughter's history, riding the fake horse on the carousel equaled major progress.

Now all he had to do was take Resa to the hospital, see about a bull, retrieve Resa postsurgery. And ignore her appeal. A tall order.

Chapter Six

"Thank you." Resa smiled at the helpful hotel clerk, then turned toward the exit. The pristine lobby gleamed with cozy seating areas and the rooms were just as welcoming. Juan was in recovery and now his wife would have a nice place near the San Antonio hospital where she could get some rest.

But there would be none of that for Resa. Not until her parents' return. Not until Colson left.

In making the move easier for Cheyenne, Resa had spent too much time with him lately, including their drive to San Antonio together this morning and the trip to the zoo. He'd always been a charmer and he was getting to her. At least once they'd arrived at the hospital, she'd been free of him until afternoon.

But now he and his daughter were waiting outside for her.

She tried to stop thinking about them, but found it difficult.

Why had Colson been so uptight on the carousel? Why had Cheyenne shut down when she'd mentioned a real horse? The child had lived on ranches her entire life. She should be comfortable with horses. Was she afraid of them? And embarrassed by her fear, since her father was a horse trainer?

Sucking in a deep breath, Resa stepped inside the moving pie slice of the revolving door, which always made her feel claustrophobic.

"Resa!"

Looking up, she spotted the two of them in the next slot, entering as she exited. A tear trickled down Cheyenne's cheek as she reached toward the glass, as her dad swept her up in his arms. Resa stayed in her pie slice until it took her back inside to them.

"Hey, sweet pea, what's wrong?"

Tears streaming, Cheyenne reached for her. "I couldn't get to you. And then I thought it was gonna eat us."

"Shh, princess." Colson handed her over. "You're safe. The door won't hurt you. And here we are. With Resa." He didn't sound pleased about that last bit.

"Those doors kind of make me nervous, too." She adjusted the child on her hip. "They suck you in and spit you out. But I've never had one chew on me."

That got a giggle out of Cheyenne, and Resa wiped away her tears.

"I take it they had a room."

"Yes."

"It's really kind of you to set Juan's wife up like this."

"He's been good to us and he'll focus on recovery better if he's not worrying about Carla. Barring complications, and if he follows his physical therapy, he's on track to come back to work in six weeks." After Cheyenne's—and Colson's—exit from her life.

Why did that put a dull ache in her chest?

"Did you eat anything? We ate, but we could stop somewhere if you need to."

Why did Colson Kincaid have to be a caring, nice guy? And why did that still do funny things to her insides?

"I'm good. I ate at the hospital cafeteria."

"Daddy?"

"Oh, right. Cheyenne needs a bathroom. That's why we came in, and then with the whole door thing, I forgot."

Resa looked around the lobby, spotted the restrooms.

"Would you mind taking her?"

"Of course not." She set Cheyenne down, took her hand—small, warm and trusting—then headed across the lobby. A welcome reprieve.

Resa enjoyed Cheyenne. But all she wanted was to get on the road, back home and away from Colson. Tomorrow, she'd hole up in her office, draft and design her day away. And avoid him.

* * *

Ideas zinged through Resa's brain all day. But yesterday's long hours had sapped her of energy. Despite the empty coffee cup on her desk, she yawned. It was well after seven, so she might as well call it a day. Friday—one workweek complete. Two more to go with Colson in her personal space.

At least tomorrow she'd be knee-deep in the store's Christmas open house, and spend half of her day away from the ranch.

After stretching as she stood, she strolled over and opened her blinds.

Cheyenne stood on the fence as before, her elbows hooked over the top rail, gazing out toward the pasture where the palomino, still heavy with colt, grazed on a bale of hay. There was no sign of Colson, but he had to be around somewhere. The little girl didn't get far from him.

Did Cheyenne want to ride? She should tell Colson it was okay, that the child could ride anytime she wanted. Resa headed for the back door and pushed it open.

But Colson was nowhere in sight. Instead Annette leaned against the barn.

"Evening. I'm sorry if we disturbed you."

"Not at all."

"Resa!" Cheyenne clambered down from the fence, ran to her.

Resa scooped her up, enjoying her pigtails and baby shampoo.

"Where's your daddy?" She scanned the area.

"He's at the house getting cleaned up from work. But I wanted to see the mama horse, so Nette brought me."

Resa turned to her. "I'm finished for the day, so you could go back and I'll bring her home in a bit."

Annette paused as if unsure, but then smiled. "I think Cheyenne would like that." She strolled toward the house.

"So, you like horses?"

Cheyenne buried her face in Resa's shoulder. "Uh-huh."

"They're so pretty. Do you want to go pet her?"

The child stiffened, shook her head, her face still hidden.

How could Cheyenne be afraid of horses when Colson had worked with them her entire life?

"You know, horses look big and scary. But they're really gentle and sweet. Especially Peaches here. I think when her baby is born, I'll name it Cream, so they can be Peaches and Cream."

Cheyenne raised up, risked a glance at the horse.

"What if we go inside the fence with her and just get a little closer, so you can see how sweet she is? I promise we won't get too close." This time.

"Okay." Cheyenne's arms tightened around her neck.

"Peaches is really calm." Resa unlatched the gate, stepped into the lot and refastened it. "Sometimes if I've had a bad day, I pet her and she soothes me."

Cheyenne didn't say anything, but her small hands clung tight. Tighter with each step Resa took.

She stopped. "I think this is close enough for today."

Cheyenne's grip relaxed slightly.

"Maybe we could go a little closer each day. And eventually you might want to pet her."

Cheyenne's cheek laid against Resa's, and she felt a heady rush at gaining the child's innocent trust.

"What are you doing?" Colson shouted.

Startled, Resa whirled around. His face was livid as he unfastened the gate. Cheyenne's grip tightened.

"We were just getting a little closer to Peaches." Resa tried to sound calm as the child started whimpering.

"Cheyenne is afraid of horses." He reached them, jerked his daughter out of her arms, stalked back to the gate. "And if anyone helps her overcome that fear, it will be me." He cuddled the girl as they exited the lot. "It's okay, sweetheart. You're safe. I'll always keep you safe."

The whimpering stopped.

"Let me take her back to the house." Annette stood by the barn, reached for the child.

"You go with Nette." Colson kissed Cheyenne's cheek. "I'll be there in a minute."

Annette shot Resa an apologetic look.

Colson glowered after them until they were out of earshot. "What were you thinking?" he barked.

"What were *you* thinking, freaking out in front of her?" Resa propped her hands on her hips. "I'd never put Cheyenne in danger. That horse is the most gentle one we have. And haven't you heard of the power of suggestion—if you tell her she's afraid of horses, she probably will be? You of all people should have her riding by now. At the rate you're going, she'll be afraid of horses her entire life."

"She's my daughter." He jammed a thumb to his chest. "My responsibility. You have no idea what she's been through. And no right to terrorize her."

"I was trying to help."

"Well, next time—just don't. Stay out of it. And stay away from Cheyenne." He stalked away, toward her parents' house.

How dare he? Resa blinked back hot tears. He wouldn't keep her away from Cheyenne. Would he?

In less than a week, how had this child wrapped her around her little finger? And Cheyenne seemed drawn to her, as well, even coming out of her shell. If he kept them apart, it would hurt them both.

She'd just have to let him cool off. Then change his mind.

Despite the bright sunshine, the wind had a bite to it. Shifting his weight from one foot to the other, Colson hesitated at the door. He shouldn't have yelled at Resa earlier. Now he'd have to come clean and reveal the thing he'd never told anyone other than his dad.

The barn door opened with enough force to fling it off its hinges, revealing a ready-for-battle Resa. Her arms were crossed over her chest, her mouth taut, her blue eyes steely, and she oozed determination from every pore.

"You can't keep me away from Cheyenne. She's just coming out of her shell and she likes me. If you don't let me see her, she might clam up again."

"You're right."

"And besides that, we're supposed to do the Singing in the Saddle in a couple of weeks."

"I said you're right."

Her mouth opened, closed. "I am."

"Yes. Can I come inside?"

She stepped back and he entered, closing the door behind him. It was a wonder it still worked.

"Is Cheyenne okay?" She sank onto a cowhide log chair.

"She's fine." With a duck of his head, he settled across from her. "No thanks to me."

"So what was that freak-out thing all about?"

"I told you how Felicity died." He ran his hand along the back of his neck, closed his eyes. "Cheyenne was watching out the window when it happened."

"Oh no."

"She saw the whole thing. Us arguing, Felicity taking off, the horse throwing her." Him cradling her lifeless body, apologizing…

"I had no idea. If I'd known, I never would have gotten her near Peaches."

"I know."

"Are you sure she's okay?"

"She's fine. She was more shaken about me grabbing her away from you than she was because of the mare."

Resa smacked her forehead and groaned. "I scared her, talking about real horses when we were on the carousel. That's why she suddenly wanted off."

"You didn't know. In fact, it was my idea for her to ride the horse on the carousel as a first step to come to terms with her fear. I should have let you in on what was happening." But he hadn't wanted to let her in his head. He didn't need her any closer than she already was.

"Can I go see her? I mean, if she sees us getting along and that she can still spend time with me, that might help. If it's okay with you?"

"It's fine. In fact, Annette's been wanting to have you over for dinner." *Please say no.* "How about tonight? Although it seems kind of odd inviting you to your parents' house." *No. Just say no.*

"I'd love to come. What should I bring?"

"Just yourself." The phone on her desk rang and he stood. Saved by the bell. "I better let you get to work."

"Thanks." She picked up the phone. "Rusticks Designs, how may I help you?" A beat or two of silence passed. "Oh no. Please don't tell me that. Is he okay?"

Colson turned to face her, finding her shoulders slumped, her forehead in her hand.

"Don't worry about the open house. I'll figure it out. Just tell him to take care of himself. And have someone disinfect his work area, okay? Thanks." She hung up. Blew out a heavy sigh.

"Everything all right?"

"Dwayne, one of the guys from the store, has the flu. He won't be able to help me with the open house tomorrow. He was supposed to work the morning shift, nine until noon. Believe it or not, Emmett promised to come and relieve me and help Tucker with the afternoon shift, so I can catch up on paperwork."

"I'll take Dwayne's shift. And if Emmett doesn't show, I'll stick around for the afternoon."

"You will?" A play of emotion ran across her features. A frown because she had to spend time with him? But then a smile, as if he were her hero.

"Of course. I'll get one of the hands to fill in at the ranch. Just tell me what you need me to do."

But if he didn't watch himself, he could get used to coming to her rescue.

Snickers pie. Why had she made Colson's favorite? Resa balanced the pie in one hand and grabbed the doorknob with the other. Wait. This was her parents' house, but they weren't home. She rang the bell instead.

The door whooshed open and Cheyenne barreled into her. Resa almost lost the pie, but the small arms stretched up around her waist would have been worth it. Especially since making Colson's favorite had been a mistake.

Intense green eyes met hers. "I think she missed you."

"I thought Daddy was gonna keep us apart."

"Nothing could make me stay away from you."

"Resa can visit you anytime, Cheyenne." But Colson's right eyebrow rose as if to say he could end it, as well. No matter what she thought about it.

Satisfied, Cheyenne let go of her and took a step back. One pigtail was fastened, the other half-done.

"Let me finish your hair now, princess."

"Okay." Cheyenne plopped down on Resa's father's favorite cowhide ottoman in the great room.

Colson settled in the accompanying chair and picked up a brush from the end table. With nimble fingers, he brushed Cheyenne's hair, separated it into three perfectly even strands and went to work on the braid. It was the most touching thing Resa had ever seen.

He caught her staring. "What? Didn't think I could do it?"

"I figured Annette was in charge of hair around here. How did you learn?"

"Daddy took me to a hairdresser and she showed

him how," Cheyenne reported. "He practiced and practiced until he got good at it."

Resa's heart warmed even more. "Ever heard of YouTube?"

"They show you how to braid hair on the internet?"

"Maybe you can look up how to French braid, Daddy?"

It was on the tip of Resa's tongue to offer, but she couldn't interrupt this sweet father-daughter time.

"We'll give it a shot."

Cheyenne's eyes went wide and she homed in on Resa. "Do you know how to French braid, Resa?"

She couldn't lie. "Actually, I do. My friend Eden and I used to do each other's."

"Can you do it for me?"

A light in Colson's eyes died. His hands stilled at the end of the braid.

"Your daddy's doing a really good job. Maybe some other time."

"But I want it French braided. And Daddy can't do that."

He unwound the braid he'd just finished, then the other completed one, and stood. "Here. You go ahead," he said, sounding as if a nail had been driven through his heart.

"How about I show your daddy how to do it for you?" Resa set the pie on the coffee table, then sat down in the chair behind the child. It smelled of her dad's Stetson cologne.

"Yes!" Cheyenne clapped her hands.

"Pull up that other stool so you can see." Resa waited until Colson scooted another ottoman over and sat down. "It's basically the same concept, but you should probably master one French braid before you try pigtails." She brushed Cheyenne's silky hair and started with two locks, leaving the rest loose.

"Only two strands?"

"You add as you go." Resa demonstrated, adding another strand, then more and more as she braided, pulling Cheyenne's hair smooth as she went. She reached the end and unwound it, then stood. "Now you try."

"I don't know about this." Colson swapped seats with her. "But I'll give it a shot."

"Start with two strands just under her crown. Good. Now, hold those with your left hand and grab another from the right. That's it. Now keep it smooth and add to this strand from the left."

"I don't have enough hands." His lips pulled taut with concentration.

"You're doing fine." Resa scooted closer, focused on the braid, smoothing the hair for him, her hand grazing his. "Just takes practice."

"Would anyone like supper?" Mac stood in the doorway, a knowing smile on his lips.

"Look, Grandpa, Resa showed Daddy how to French braid my hair."

"I see that. I didn't think you could get any prettier, but you just keep surprising me."

Colson painstakingly finished the braid and Resa handed him the coated rubber band to secure it. When he'd finished, she smoothed a few strands and poked them underneath.

"You'll be a pro before you know it," she told him.

Cheyenne jumped up. "Let's go show Nette, Grandpa."

"Lead the way, dumplin'." Mac took the child's hand. "Y'all come on. Food's ready."

Colson hesitated, caught Resa's gaze. "Thanks for including me."

"I figured it would be easier than me coming over every morning." She shoved her hands in her pockets.

"I worry about…losing her." Vulnerability put a sheen in his eyes, a catch in his voice. "About someone else taking my place in her heart."

"Are you kidding me? She adores you."

"You know the way." He retrieved her pie, held a hand out, ushering Resa in front of him.

Why would Colson worry about losing Cheyenne? And how could she take up residence in the little girl's heart when Cheyenne and her dad would be leaving in just over two weeks?

Eleven thirty and a lull had finally hit. It always amazed Colson at the new items Rusticks offered. The Christmas tree behind them decorated with hand-carved items was almost bare. Despite numerous sales, with a steady stream of customers all day at their open house, tables still held a picked-over display.

Log snowmen and owls, walking sticks, tree-stump-slice chessboards, log lamps and candleholders. Along with a dozen or so of Jed's boxes. Yes, Colson had trained and worked as a crafter years ago. But coming up with unique ideas and designs was beyond him.

That was Resa's expertise. She scanned the table, moved a lamp here and there to fill in the gaps of their pilfered exhibit.

"Have you heard from Emmett?" He kept his tone casual.

"No, but I'm still hoping." She blew out a big breath. "I really don't know what happened with him. We used to be close. He was a good kid, who loved church just as much as I did. Somewhere along the way he changed. During his teen years, he became a different person—so self-absorbed. I pray for him. And I know God's bigger than Emmett, but I'm losing hope for him to ever change."

"There's always hope." Colson touched her arm. She stiffened until he let his hand fall away.

"If he doesn't show, I'll stay."

"You need to get home and enjoy the rest of your cattle-free day with Cheyenne." Resa lowered her voice. "Did you French braid her hair this morning?"

"I did. Not as well as you, but Annette helped

smooth it out and tuck some ends in. By the way, you don't have to tell any of the ranch hands I do her hair."

"Your secret's safe with me." Resa chuckled.

His gut twisted. If only she knew his real secret.

She scrutinized him, as if he'd shown his discomfort, then turned back to the display. "You should have brought Cheyenne. I always loved helping my dad set up for open house. Emmett, too. Dad always said we were his best salesman."

"She's still not good with big crowds." And he couldn't risk her being around Emmett if he showed up.

"I'm really sorry about yesterday." Resa winced. "She didn't have any nightmares, did she?"

"No. She's fine. Really. All she can think about is Singing in the Saddle."

"Does she know a horse will be pulling the wagon?"

"Not yet. I'll explain before then. But I won't force her."

"Of course not. Maybe it will help her fear. She really needs to overcome it—I mean, with her being raised on ranches."

"I know." He hadn't meant for his response to sound so clipped. Resa was only trying to help. But this relationship she was building with Cheyenne—the niece she didn't know she had—was about to undo him.

Silence hung between them, as if she was choosing her words carefully. "Does she remember? I mean, when…"

"She saw a therapist for a while. The psychologist seemed to think she doesn't actually remember the horse throwing Felicity, since she was so small at the time." The muscle in his jaw throbbed. "Cheyenne only knows her mom died and she's afraid of horses."

"Maybe taking her out in the lot with a gentle animal like I did yesterday might help. A little farther each day. Then getting her to pet the horse. And eventually ride."

"Maybe. But if anyone does that with her, it'll be me." He pinned Resa with an uncompromising stare.

She raised both palms in a conciliatory gesture. "Once you get her past her fears, I could ride double with her. If that's okay with you."

"I'll think about it."

"I'm here." Emmett strolled toward them, checked his Rolex. "And I'm even early."

The hair on the back of Colson's neck prickled. Even though Cheyenne was with his dad and Annette.

Resa's eyes widened, reflecting shock that he'd actually shown up. "I'm so proud of you." She hugged her brother as he stepped around a table.

"I'll get out of here now." Colson would like to offer to stay until Tucker came. But what if Dad decided to bring Cheyenne for a visit? Resa didn't see herself in Cheyenne when she looked at his little girl, but would that be the case with Emmett if he got a glimpse of her? Colson couldn't let that happen.

Chapter Seven

"Thanks for helping us out." Resa watched Colson grab his coat. Thankfully, Emmett had shown up, relieving her of Colson's presence. It had been too much like that summer he'd worked at the ranch. Back when part of her heart had died before it ever got a chance to truly blossom.

"Well, look who's here." Ronald Ashford, local radio personality, stopped in front of their booth, recorder in hand. "All three heirs of Rusticks Log Furnishings in one place. This screams for an interview."

Colson stopped, reluctance in his stiff stance.

"That's really not necessary." Resa's nerves simply couldn't handle anything else.

"But isn't this open house thing set up to advertise the stores?" Ronald splayed his hands. "What better way to accomplish that than free radio time?"

A valid point. She stifled a sigh. "How long will it take?"

"A matter of minutes. Right here. Right now."

"Now?" A minute to pull herself together would be nice.

"As soon as Mr. Kincaid comes back. Come on, help me out. My station manager is whining for a human interest piece."

Resa glanced over at Colson. "Do you mind?"

"I reckon, but I've only got a minute." Colson stiffly leaned his hip against a table, as if he couldn't wait to get away from her.

Ronald counted down with his fingers, then pointed at them. "This is Ronald Ashford with KTLB at the Christmas open house at Rusticks Log Furniture in the heart of Texas Hill Country. I'm here with Emmett and Resa McCall, grandchildren of Emmerson and Teresa McCall, who founded Rusticks. I also have Colson Kincaid, son of Mackenzie Kincaid, who's been in partnership with the McCall family for the last ten years. Tell me, Resa, how did the McCalls and Kincaids end up in business together?"

"Well, my grandfather started out handcrafting furniture for family and friends, to make ends meet on a pastor's salary." She grew more at ease as she shared her family legacy. "Word of mouth about his skill traveled fast. Jed Whitlow was the first crafter he trained, and his lifelong friend Henry Kincaid was able to help them keep up for a while. They started the Bandera store fifty years ago. My father grew up in the workshop and soaked up Grandpa's skills."

A few people gathered in a semicircle to listen.

"How did the San Antonio store come about?" Ronald held the recorder in front of Colson.

"My grandfather Henry taught my dad everything he knew, so when they started getting a lot of orders from San Antonio clients, they decided to expand. By then my grandfather and the older McCalls had retired, The younger McCalls stayed in Bandera, and Dad agreed to move to San Antonio and run the store there."

The semicircle around them grew, comprised mostly of women. Probably drawn by the two handsome men flanking Resa, more than their story.

"I didn't think you worked in the store. Didn't you run off to travel the rodeo or something?"

"I didn't run off, just followed my dream." Colson's jaw tensed. "I was a horse trainer at King's Ranch in Kingsville for a while, and I'm currently the ranch foreman there. But I'm here for a short time while the McCalls' foreman has surgery."

"Rusticks advertises handmade furnishings from Texas trees. Just how handmade are we talking?"

"When Rusticks began, everything was done by hand. But to keep up with demand, we do use machinery to cut tenons, drilling and sanding. However, Resa and another drafter design all of our furnishings, and all pieces are assembled by hand."

Ronald jabbed the microphone at Emmett. "Tell us how the trees are harvested."

Did Emmett know how to handle the question,

to appease environmentalists? Resa resisted the urge to cut in.

"The original furnishings came from trees on my grandfather's property. In the years since, we maintain our own forest for Rusticks. When a tree is cut down, we plant one in its place. We also provide the service of tree removal for new construction, cutting limbs off trees around homes, or harvesting trees that have fallen. Just call us and our crew will take care of your tree problems for free, in exchange for the wood."

He did know. Wow, he'd actually paid attention when they were growing up.

"Rusticks helps with oak wilt problems, as well. If you discover a diseased tree, call us." Emmett quoted their number. "We'll harvest the tree and use whatever wood we can. And the utility companies contact us when they cut limbs along power lines."

Resa worked at keeping her jaw from dropping at his knowledge of a company he'd shown nothing but disinterest in over the years.

"Now about the store... Do you take custom orders?" Ronald focused on her again.

"Yes." She rattled off the address and contact information. "We have a showroom full of unique furniture and decor items for every space in your house, along with staff to help with special orders. If you or I can imagine it, we can craft it."

Ronald scanned the store. "Tell us about the hand-carved canes."

"Anyone who lives in Bandera or has visited the area has probably seen Jed Whitlow. He sits on the pew outside Rusticks almost every day." She couldn't talk about him without smiling. "As I said, he was the first crafter my grandfather hired. After he retired from full-time work, he kept carving for us."

She picked up a cane and gestured to the table holding the rest of Jed's work. "He does walking canes for us, along with candlesticks, table lamps, Christmas ornaments and, his newest item, cedar jewelry boxes. We're hoping to have some of his hope chests soon."

"There you have it, folks. Come to Rusticks for all your log furnishing needs, tree removal services and conversation pieces. This is Ronald Ashford at the Rusticks Furniture open house in the heart of Texas Hill Country." He stopped the recorder. "Thanks, guys."

"Thank you." Resa set the cane down.

"I'm interested in a jewelry box." A woman gave Colson a flirty smile, obviously interested in more than furniture.

"I'm sorry, I have an important appointment. But Resa can help you." He made for the door, but the woman stepped in his path.

"Jed, the crafter, can engrave a name on a silver plate for the side if you'd like." Resa opened a jewelry box to show the woman the tray inside, attempting to distract her. "At no extra charge."

"Can you deliver it personally?" The woman practically batted her eyelashes at Colson.

"Sorry, but I don't make deliveries." He sidestepped her, heading purposely for the door.

Hmm. Apparently, he wasn't interested. Still grieving Felicity.

After one more lingering perusal of Colson, the woman turned to Emmett.

"I'll make deliveries," he offered smoothly.

"Actually, he won't be around to do so." Resa pasted on a smile. "But we will deliver."

The woman lost interest and sashayed away. But three others stepped forward, eager to check out the jewelry boxes.

After making a sale, Resa glanced up to see Tucker Dobson hobbling their way. A longtime salesman for Rusticks, he'd been with them almost as long as Jed.

"Sorry." He tipped his cowboy hat. "Nina had to spray me down with Lysol before she let me in the store. Sure as shootin', she got me coming and going for two days now, making sure nobody gets Dwayne's flu."

She grinned, then kissed his weathered cheek. "Sure as shootin' I gotta go." She hurried to the exit, checking her watch. A few minutes until noon. If she could keep her mind off a certain cowboy, she'd get several hours in at her office. But staying focused was a challenge these days.

Given the choice of a singles' or men's only Sunday school class, Colson had chosen the men's. He had no clue which class Resa attended, but just in case she went with the singles, he wanted to give her space. There was no reason to force his presence on her any more than necessary.

When class was dismissed, chair legs scraped against the floor as everyone stood and pushed away from the long table. Chase helped him find his way through the maze. He'd attended a handful of times, but that was almost six years ago.

"Some folks gather in the fellowship hall for a quick cup of coffee, or you can go on to the sanctuary."

"I had two cups before I ever made it here, so I'm good on caffeine."

"I'm short, so I'll see you in a bit."

"Where do I find Cheyenne?"

"More than likely Marilyn will bring her to you. You know your way back to the sanctuary from here?"

"I'm good. Thanks."

Chase strolled away. Apparently he didn't know Colson's story. Or he was more forgiving than Resa.

"Daddy!" Cheyenne let go of Marilyn's hand and ran toward him. The delight in her face sent a thrill through him. How long had it been since she'd been excited about something?

She barreled into him. "Guess who was in my class?"

"Miss Marilyn?"

"No, silly. Ruby. My new friend. Can I sit with her and her parents?"

"Oh, I don't know, princess. We don't really know her folks and they may not be up for that."

Ruby headed his way, holding hands with a woman who stuck her free hand toward him. "I'm Scarlet Miller, Ruby's mom. We'd love to have Cheyenne sit with us during the service if you don't mind."

He clasped her hand.

Marilyn shot him a wink. "I'll vouch for Scarlet and Drew. She comes from good stock—Scarlet's daddy, Ron, has worked at the Chasing Eden Dude Ranch for years. They'll keep an eye on Cheyenne here and make sure she doesn't giggle during the sermon."

"If you sit with Ruby—" he knelt at eye level with Cheyenne "—you have to be quiet and still. You can't decide you want to sit with me and move during the sermon. You can't get up and go to the bathroom or anywhere else, either. And absolutely no whispering, giggling or wiggling."

"I promise I'll be good, Daddy."

"I'll take them both to the water fountain and the bathroom before we go into the sanctuary." Marilyn clasped Ruby's hand. "And the Millers will keep them in line during the sermon."

"Okay."

Small arms wrapped around his neck. "Thanks, Daddy."

She happily left him there, and Colson's heart sank. Cheyenne needed this. To stop clinging to him. To make friends her age. So why did it hurt him so? She was growing up before his eyes.

He stood and strolled toward the sanctuary. The long hallway had cleared, but he heard voices. He was sure one of them was Resa's.

Colson stopped.

"...I have to admit, I didn't think you'd come. But I'm so glad you did."

"I'm trying to get my life back on track." Emmett sounded contrite. "I thought me coming this morning might help."

Emmett was here? Colson's chest tightened. The urge to blast past them, grab Cheyenne and flee welled within him. But then Emmett might see them together. And know? Maybe it was better that she was sitting with her new friend this morning. Maybe God had worked that out for him. Yeah, right, God helping him keep his secret? God loved truth. Guilt pooled hot in Colson's stomach.

"Still the fourth row, right side." A tinge of bitterness edged Emmett's words.

"You remembered?"

"Everything about this place is etched into me."

"That's not a bad thing."

"I just remember being dragged here every time the doors were open."

"You used to love church." The sad lilt of her tone tugged at Colson.

"Maybe if they'd let up a little. Stopped forcing me. Let me come on my own."

"You probably wouldn't have ever darkened the door if they'd done that."

"You're right." Emmett laughed. "You go on. I'll be right behind you."

Feeling like an eavesdropper, Colson stepped through the foyer just as Resa entered the sanctuary.

Emmett leaned against the wall to the side of the double doors, eyes closed. Nautical polo shirt, loafers... Pure preppy.

Had he really turned over a new leaf? Colson hoped so, for Resa's sake. For Cheyenne's sake. But if so, why was he hesitant to enter the sanctuary? If Emmett was trying to pull one over on Resa, to take advantage of her, Colson would be there to call him on it.

Ice-blue eyes opened, issuing a challenge as Emmett straightened. "Stay away from her."

"Hard to do since I'm overseeing the ranch."

"You better not hurt her again."

"Don't intend to." Colson shoved his hands in his pockets. "I'm just here to work."

"Hurt her again and you answer to me." Emmett

jabbed a thumb at his chest, then slipped through the door, as if he thought Colson might take him up on his challenge.

Colson wasn't falling for this upstanding-citizen, hardworking, protective-brother routine. He would keep an eye on Emmett. If anyone had the capacity to hurt Resa, it would be her brother.

If anyone had the capacity to hurt Cheyenne, it was her biological father.

Members gathered at the altar went back to their seats, the hymn wound down and the pastor offered the closing prayer. Amens echoed and her brother was the first one out of the pew. Just like when they were teenagers. At least he'd come.

"Hey, wait up."

"What?" Emmett stopped, glanced around as if he couldn't get out of there fast enough.

"I thought we might do lunch. It's not every Sunday I get to sit in church with my brother. Let me do one thing and then we'll go." Resa searched for Jed. She couldn't wait to tell him about the jewelry boxes.

"Um, I never agreed to lunch."

"You're coming." She spotted her quarry. "Hey, Jed, I've got good news and bad news."

"Just give it to me straight." He pulled Marilyn to his side. "Only sold one, huh? Or none?"

"We sold them all."

"All of them?" Marilyn let out a whoop.

Jed's smile broadened, but then he frowned. "So what's the bad news?"

"We need more. Fast. At the moment I have orders for a dozen."

"By doggie's, I'm not sure I can keep up with that."

"You have to," Resa begged. "I want to take some to the trade show this weekend, too."

"We'll figure something out." Marilyn patted his shoulder and caught Resa's gaze. "Can the crafters at Rusticks make boxes?"

"That's a great idea." Emmett butted into the conversation. "Those things sold like hotcakes."

"But we wouldn't want to cut into Jed's market," Resa cautioned.

"He could sell us the design?"

"Better yet, we could use Jed's design and take a commission," Resa mused. "The ones we craft could have stickers that say Designed by Jed Whitlow. But the boxes you make would say Handcrafted by Jed Whitlow—with a bigger price, and you get all of the profits."

"Wait a minute." Emmett glowered.

"Reckon your folks will be okay with that?"

"You know they will. And besides, I'm in charge at the moment." She shot Emmett a look.

"Sounds like you got yourself a deal." Jed stuck his hand out. "But when your folks get back, run it by them to make sure, you hear?"

Resa hugged him instead of shaking hands.

"Better than any handshake." Marilyn joined in the embrace. "Let's celebrate. Y'all join us at OST."

"What's OST?" Emmett frowned.

"Old Spanish Trail. Remember?" Resa linked arms with him. "You really have been gone too long."

"How about you, Colson?" Marilyn looked past Resa.

She hadn't even realized he was still around. But there he was, leaning against a pew behind them.

Colson stiffened. "I'm not sure I can."

Because of her? Did he agree they'd been getting along too well, spending too much time together lately?

"You should come." Marilyn patted his arm. "Cheyenne would love it. Where is she? I was thinking we could invite Ruby and her folks, too."

His gaze cut to Emmett. "Bathroom."

"Resa." Jed shot her a wink. "You coming?"

Think of an excuse. But she didn't have any and she couldn't disappoint Jed. "Sure. But you're not paying for my meal. In fact, I have a check for you from the open house sales. Along with a list of buyers wanting their engraved plates."

"My devious plan worked." Jed twisted his make-believe mustache. "We'll hash out who's buying when we get there. See who wins. You coming, Emmett?"

"Thanks, but I've already got lunch plans."

She saw Colson immediately relax. Maybe it was

Emmett he didn't want to spend time with. But why? They'd never been friends, but they weren't enemies, either.

She gave Jed a good-natured grin, then headed for her car, but Emmett caught her elbow.

"Since when do we do business on a handshake, much less a hug? What about a contract and why are you giving away our profit potential?"

"Most people would require a contract. But not Jed." She rolled her eyes. "He's an honorable man. And much of our early profits came from the sweat of his brow. These boxes are his design and we're not stealing his retirement income from him. His arthritis is bad enough that he could easily get disability, but he wants to earn his living. And I'll do everything I can to help him do that."

"Whatever you say." A muscle tic started up in Emmett's jaw. "You're the one in charge." He marched out.

And she wanted to jerk a knot in his tail. She huffed out a harsh breath, then strolled to the lobby. Emmett had more interest in the company these days, but he was entirely too wrapped up in profit. They had plenty of income without stealing from Jed.

She shook hands with the pastor and exited.

Halfway across the parking lot, she heard footfalls catching up with her.

"Resa. Wait up." Cheyenne skipped up beside

her. "Daddy said we can go to OST. And Ruby might come, too."

"I'm so glad you made a new friend." Had Colson changed his mind because Emmett wasn't going? "What about Mac and Annette?"

"Them, too."

"Yay!" Resa cheered and got a giggle out of Cheyenne.

"Can Ruby ride with us, Daddy?"

"Why don't you go ask her folks."

Cheyenne galloped toward the Millers.

"That was awesome." Colson's gaze was full of…something she couldn't read. But it threatened to warm her heart.

"What?"

"You making that deal with Jed. You could have gotten a lot more out of it. And the way you stood up to Emmett was heroic."

"I don't know about that." She chuckled. "Jed's been good to us. We try to return the favor." What was she doing, pitting herself against her brother? Taking sides with Colson? And why did his approval make her feel so warm inside?

Chapter Eight

Colson's boots made a racket as he crossed the hardwood floor of the restaurant. Cheyenne, his dad and Annette had all ganged up on him to come. So much for nipping things between his daughter and her aunt. For today, anyway.

The place hadn't changed a bit. Servers ducked under the enormous elk behind the breakfast bar, which was still lined by saddle-topped stools. The salad bar was housed in a covered wagon, the John Wayne Room's walls crammed with pictures and memorabilia.

Resa reached a long table where Jed and Marilyn waited, and settled in a chair. Cheyenne clambered into the one beside her, then patted the other flanking her for Colson.

"Where's Ruby?" Resa helped scoot Cheyenne's chair in.

"She couldn't come. They had lunch plans with her grandparents." Cheyenne's lips turned down.

"Maybe she can come next time."

An instrumental song started up. It was Annette's ringtone, "Music Box Dancer."

"Excuse me." She fished around in her purse, dug out her phone. "Hello?" She smiled. "Yes, that's perfect. I'll see you both then." Annette clicked off, turned to Cheyenne. "Guess who's coming to visit Tuesday?"

"Who?" The little girl's forehead scrunched.

"Ruby. I asked her mom this morning when Ruby could come. She's gonna bring her over and let her stay with us all day."

Cheyenne showed a mixture of joy and worry— a smile followed by another frown. "What for?"

"To play."

"What will we do?"

"Whatever you want." Annette reached across the table to squeeze Cheyenne's hand. "Don't be shy. You and Ruby liked sitting together at church. You'll have fun."

"Okay."

"Isn't it nice of Annette to arrange this, princess?" Colson winked at her.

"Thanks, Nette." But Cheyenne still didn't sound so sure.

"You need to make friends your own age instead of being stuck with old codgers like us all the time." Mac gently tugged her braid.

"You're not an old codger, Grandpa. And Nette's not, too."

"Then that must make me a spring chicken." Colson opened his menu.

"Look at the tree, Daddy."

Decked out with cowboy boot ornaments, red stars and balls, with a rope wound around it instead of garland, topped with a bandana and a cowboy hat, the tree almost reached the ceiling.

"Can we get a tree and decorate it like that?"

Daddy failure. He hadn't even thought about a tree.

"I can't believe I didn't think of that." Resa closed her menu, set it down. "My parents were so busy getting ready for their cruise, I told them I'd decorate after they left. After lunch, I'll stop by and dig the tree and ornaments out of the attic. I'm sure we can find a hat, bandana and rope lying around."

"But Daddy always cuts a real tree for us. We go out in the woods and find the perfect one."

"Then that's what we'll do." Resa patted Cheyenne's hand.

"We don't want to be any trouble." He tried to concentrate on the menu. "We can use an artificial one this time."

"But I've never gone out in the woods and picked a real one." Her wonder was childlike, her eyes sparkling, a look he couldn't resist. "It sounds fun."

"Can we, Daddy?"

"I guess so, if Resa's certain she doesn't mind."

She looked at the others around the table. "Anybody else want to come?"

"I've got some sewing to do." Marilyn sipped her tea.

"My recliner's calling me." Jed set his menu down.

"Mine, too." Mac chuckled.

"I just bought a new book by my favorite author." Annette rubbed her hands together. "I can't wait to dive in."

"I guess it's just the three of us then." Regret tinged her tone, as if she wished she hadn't gotten so excited about the tree.

Did she want to put the brakes on things between them, too?

Stomach in knots, the way it always was when Colson was around, Resa traipsed through the woods with him and Cheyenne. She'd imagined Mac and Annette in on the trek when she'd suggested it. Why hadn't she kept her mouth shut?

"What about that one?" She pointed at an ash juniper, the Texas version of cedar.

Cheyenne wrinkled her nose. "Too weird shaped."

"It'll be hard to find a perfect-shaped one around here, since we don't get much rain except in spring. But we can trim it."

"I wanna keep looking until we find the perfect one."

"Resa may not have that much time, princess."

"Just as long as we get back in time for evening church, I'm good." Resa squeezed the little girl's hand. "Wanna walk the log across the river?"

"I'm not sure that's a good idea." Colson eyed the water.

"It's not deep here. And it's not that cold. I wouldn't suggest it if there was any danger." When would he ever learn she'd never do anything to harm Cheyenne?

"Can we, Daddy?"

"I reckon." He clasped Cheyenne's free hand.

"Here we go." Resa stepped up on the log.

Cheyenne followed, then Colson, in single file.

When they reached the end, Cheyenne squealed. "That was fun, Daddy. Swing me."

"Resa will have to help. On three?" His gaze met hers. "One, two, three."

They swung Cheyenne up in the air, their laughter mixing with her gleeful giggles. Like a family.

"Again."

They swung her three more times.

"You're getting big. And Resa's arm is probably tired."

Piles and piles of tree trunks, logs, branches and roots occupied the clearing, encompassing everything from river-whitened cypress to black walnut.

Cheyenne grew wide-eyed as they neared the log yard. "What happened to all these trees?"

"We either grew them for furniture, they died on someone else's property, a family needed them cut so they could build a house, or they got sick. They're waiting to be made into furniture. But there's a nice grove over there."

Cheyenne had already spotted it. "There." She tugged them toward a tree. "I want that one."

"I think this will work nicely." Colson walked in a slow circle around the tree. "It's nice and tall."

"It's even taller than you." Cheyenne inspected its height, at least a head above Colson.

He set down his backpack, pulled out a chain saw. "Cover your ears, princess."

"Come sit with me." Resa tested a log pile, then sat, helping Cheyenne onto her lap.

"Don't snakes hide under logs?"

"It's about fifty degrees, so they're way down in the ground. If it gets to be sixty, we'll be more careful." She clasped Cheyenne's hands and clamped them over the child's ears as the whir of the chain saw started up.

Colson made quick work cutting the tree, and minutes later, he leaned it against a live oak and strolled over to them. "You know what that means?" His attention was fixed on Cheyenne.

"Bonfire time. With s'mores."

"I'm not sure that's a good idea. We might be under a burn ban," Resa said. "And I didn't bring any supplies. But I have snacks back at the house."

"I'm not into starting forest fires. I've got this." Colson dug around in his backpack, pulled out a bag of marshmallows, a box of graham crackers and several Hershey chocolate bars, along with matches. And finally, a small camping-style grill and a jug of water. "I do need skewers, though."

"There's a scrap pile at the east corner of the pole yard."

"I'm on it." Colson set the grill down, lit the charcoal, then walked away.

Minutes later, he returned with three long, slim branches, settled on a log nearby and shaved skewers for each of them. He slid a marshmallow onto each stick and handed them over.

"Want me to roast yours for you?" Cheyenne asked Resa, scooting out of her lap.

"Sounds like you're the pro. But do yours first."

While Resa readied the crackers and chocolate, the child kept the marshmallow just out of the fire until it turned a golden brown on all sides. They carefully slid the marshmallow in place and set the s'more on a paper plate to cool, while Cheyenne went back to roasting. Colson poured coffee for them and hot chocolate for Cheyenne from thermoses.

He'd come prepared, a ritual they obviously shared every Christmas. Only this time, Resa was included. Like a family. But she couldn't let herself get entangled with Colson. Not when he was leaving. Again.

"Yum." Resa sipped her coffee. "What else do you have in that awesome bag?"

"That's about it."

Minutes later, they were all sticky and giggling as Resa licked chocolate from her lips.

With the sun in her eyes, Cheyenne squinted up at her. "I wish you were my mommy."

And Resa's stomach did a flip. Her gaze darted

to Colson. He seemed as much at a loss on how to respond as she was.

"You have a mommy. She's just in heaven now."

"But I don't remember her anymore. And I need a mommy here."

"Well, I'd love to be your friend. Maybe like a special aunt."

Something splattered and the fire sizzled. "Better get back to the house if we're gonna decorate the tree." Colson's words were gruff as he poured water on the flames. Smoke billowed and the fire died.

She could have sat here with them all day. But he was right, if they were gonna decorate the tree and make evening services, they needed to go. She stood, brushed off the seat of her jeans.

"What about the grill?"

"I'll come back for it after it cools."

But she couldn't help thinking his sudden desire for departure had something to do with the developing bond between her and Cheyenne. As if he didn't want her getting too close.

Maybe he was right. They were leaving, after all.

And why did her heart break a little at the thought? Because of Cheyenne, or her cowboy daddy?

"I love these ornaments, don't you, Daddy?"

"I do." He slipped a cross onto the tree. He loved decorating the tree with Cheyenne. Just not with

Resa. He'd assumed once they cut the tree, she'd go home. He'd been wrong.

"My family always has star, angel and cross ornaments to symbolize Jesus." Resa noticed the ornament he'd placed. "Wait, we have to put the lights on first."

"Oh yeah." He removed the cross, set it back in the box with the others.

"Did Mr. Jed make all these wooden ones?"

"Some of them. My dad and grandfather carved some, too." Resa untangled the last length of lights. "You wanna see how my brother and I used to put the lights on?"

Colson swallowed hard at the mention of Emmett. "Uh-huh." Cheyenne nodded.

"Wrap them around me."

"Huh?"

"If you try to hold them all out straight and go around and around the tree, they end up tangled again. This way they don't. And besides, this way is more fun." Resa clamped her arms to her sides and spread her feet apart. "Go ahead, wrap them around me."

"You sure about this?"

Resa looked up at him. "Works great, trust me. To be honest, the first time, Emmett did it to torment me. But after he got in trouble, as he untwirled me he wound the lights around the tree. It worked like a charm, so we did it that way every year until my parents got a prelit artificial tree when I was ten. We usually use these for the roof."

"Do we put them all in a clump?" Cheyenne made a circle around Resa, winding lights around her.

"Kind of spiral them up and down my legs, then as high as you can reach. They can be pretty tight and I'll still be able to walk."

Cheyenne skipped in circles around her, giggling as she went, effectively swathing Resa with Christmas lights.

"Good job." Resa laughed. "I'd high-five you if I could. Come to think of it, maybe I should have held my arms up, so I could still use them. Oh well." She shuffled over to the tree, completely unselfconscious, with her arms strapped to her sides from her elbows down. "Okay, now unwind me and we'll circle the tree as we go."

"You look like a Christmas light mummy." Colson leaned his shoulder against a wall. Or the perfect gift wrapped in twinkly lights.

"Or a Christmas tree dummy." She grinned. "No pictures, please. I do not want to see this posted anywhere."

"Daddy says never to call anybody a dummy." Cheyenne unwound a length of lights. "Not even yourself."

Resa closed her eyes, sufficiently chastened. "Your father is right. Forget I said that."

Cheyenne tugged on the lights and Resa bobbled slightly.

"Easy. Need help?" He didn't want to get too close to her, but this looked like it could get dangerous. He imagined Cheyenne tugging too hard or fast, unwinding Resa like a spinning top. His daughter probably didn't have the strength, but Resa could get dizzy if Cheyenne went too fast.

"Maybe while Cheyenne untwirls me, you can help place the lights—artfully."

"Artfully?"

"You know, where they kind of swag up and down."

"Swag?"

"Like this, Daddy." Cheyenne unwound a section of lights from Resa, placed them on the tree in an intricate swag formation.

"That's perfect, Cheyenne. You're really good at this. I'm not picky, but they just look kind of odd if they're in a straight line."

The three of them moved slowly around the tree, placing lights just so, unwinding Resa as they went, with a constant stream of giggles from Cheyenne. Few adults would go to such lengths to entertain a child. But then Resa had always been down-to-earth, had never put on airs. There was nothing haughty about her, unlike his mom, or Felicity. That's why he'd fallen for her. Why she terrified him now.

Their progress stopped. He looked down at Cheyenne, whose head was bent at Resa's knees.

"Uh-oh. The lights are tangled."

"Can you get it?" Resa stood still, patiently.

"Can you help, Daddy?" Cheyenne stepped back out of the way.

He was getting too close. He knelt, tugged at the strands. Two bulbs were tangled together, and he worked to free them, his fingers brushing the fabric of her jeans. Thankfully, she didn't wear those second-skin kind.

"There you go." He stood.

Resa let out a slow breath, as if she'd been holding it. "That was a close one. I thought I was gonna be a Christmas mummy forever." She winked at Cheyenne.

Why did she take his breath away?

Because she was Resa. Tenderhearted, kind, fun. Because she'd paid more attention to Cheyenne since they'd been here than Felicity ever had. Because around her, his heart beat in a way it never had around his wife.

Cheyenne started circling the tree again, unraveling Resa.

He chuckled.

"What?"

He couldn't seem to stop laughing as she slowly spun around. The rest of the lights uncoiled without incident.

Finally free, Resa grabbed a heavy rope with

a lasso at the end. Again, she let Cheyenne coil it around her, then painstakingly spun in circles to unwind it onto the tree until he slipped the loop over the top branches.

"Ready for some color?" She opened a tub of red ball ornaments, each nested in a rounded compartment.

"Pretty!" Cheyenne did a little bounce.

"Careful, if you drop these, they'll break." Resa made sure Cheyenne had a good hold on the wire hook attached to the ball before she let go.

Cheyenne hung the ornament on a branch, then stood back and looked at it with wonder. "Put the bandana and the hat on, Daddy."

"Sure thing, princess." He tied the red bandana high up in the tree and set the hat on top, as if it was shading a cowboy's face.

"That's perfect." Cheyenne clapped her hands. "Now we need lots of ornaments."

"Why don't you hang the wooden ones?" he suggested. "They're my favorites." The crosses, stars and angels symbolized Jesus in rustic simplicity. And they didn't break. No worries about sliced fingers.

"Mine, too." Cheyenne went to work on the wooden ornaments.

A few minutes later, the tree was all decked out, with few empty branches to be found.

"That looks wonderful," Colson's dad exclaimed, as he and Annette entered the room.

"We had so much fun." Cheyenne scampered to them. "I wrapped Resa up in Christmas lights and then untwirled her to put them on the tree. We did the rope that way, too."

Dad chuckled. "I don't think I've ever decorated a tree like that, but it sounds fun. It's almost time for evening church. Better get ready, munchkin."

"Wow, I had no idea it was getting so late." Resa checked the clock on the mantel. "I better get home and freshen up."

"Thanks, Resa." Cheyenne darted back and gave her a big hug.

"You're welcome, sweet pea. That's the most fun I've had decorating a tree since I was ten."

"Let's go get your dress on." Annette led Cheyenne to the stairs, and Dad followed.

Suddenly alone with Resa, Colson felt awkward.

"I'll put the storage tubs back in the attic," she said.

"Don't worry, I'll get them."

"Okay then." She shoved her hands in her pockets. "See you later."

As she turned away, headed for the front door, the thing most prevalent on his mind was how good today felt, how he wanted to spend every Christmas like this. With Resa.

This was bad. This was very bad.

Chapter Nine

A yawn escaped as Resa descended the stairs, running her hand down the smooth surface of the twisted, gnarled cedar railing as she went. One cowboy-inspired tree, a happy little girl and an evening church service later, she'd fallen into bed and slept like a log. But her alarm had gone off way too early this morning.

"There you are." Emmett was sprawled on the couch in the den.

She squealed, clutched a hand to her chest. "What are you doing here?"

"Trying to spend time with my sister."

"It's Monday. I have to work, and I thought you left after morning service yesterday." Her gaze narrowed. Emmett? Wanting to hang with her? What was he up to? "Your car wasn't here when I got back last night."

"I got in late. Tried not to disturb you. Guess it worked."

"But you're always dying to get back to Dallas."

"Just thought I'd stick around. See how you're doing with Mom and Dad gone."

"I'm fine."

"I've got a hankering for French toast. Want some?"

Her stomach promptly growled. "Yum."

"Then allow me." He stood, ushered her to the back part of the house. "I couldn't find any bacon. Or sausage, for that matter."

"There's bacon right here." She opened the fridge, fished the package out of the drawer.

"Turkey bacon?" His lip curled. "That's not what I had in mind."

"Have you ever even tried it?" She set the bacon on the counter, poured a cup of coffee and took her seat at the island breakfast bar across from the stove.

"Negative." He dug in the fridge, came out with butter, eggs and milk.

"Cook me up some and you can give it a taste."

"I'll cook it for you, but I'll pass on the taste test." He dropped a generous blob of butter into a skillet, whisked the eggs, dipped slices of bread in the goo and laid them in the pan. Then separated the turkey strips and set them to sizzling in another skillet.

"You're not really here to fix me breakfast. Spill."

He tucked his bottom lip between his teeth. "Did Dad ever mention moving our corporate offices to San Antonio?"

"What?"

"No offense, but some of us think our corporate offices are outgrowing that shack where the factory is."

"That *shack* is an impressive, massive log structure our grandfather built." She reached for her coffee, but her hand shook. Maybe she'd had enough caffeine.

"Precisely my point." He sprinkled cinnamon over the toast. "We need to move into the next century."

"We're right in the middle of town, where our grandparents built our reputation. What site could possibly be better for this business than right where we are?"

He calmly flipped each bacon slice. "Not the store. Or the factory. Just corporate sales and designs. We're a thriving business. We shouldn't be stuck in an ancient store with our designer in a barn."

Resa frowned. "San Antonio is an hour away. And I'm inspired right where my office is."

"Most companies don't house their offices with the store and factory. We could have skyscraper offices with nice views. Especially if we take our stock public."

"Public?" She shook her head. "That's not the vision Mom and Dad have. Rusticks has always been down-to-earth. A family business."

"It was just an idea. We can discuss it further after you've had time to think on it."

"No further discussion is needed. Our corporate

offices aren't going anywhere. And our stock won't go public. Why would you even think I'd consider such a thing?"

Emmett's mouth clamped shut as he flipped the toast, then glanced up at the picture of their parents. "It was Dad's idea."

Resa's jaw dropped.

"But Mom disagreed. She's always so overly cautious, while Dad's a bit more adventurous. Which is where every argument they've ever had during their entire marriage has stemmed from. Maybe you could talk to Mom."

"No. I'm not talking to Mom. She's right."

"So you're taking sides?"

"You are, too."

"Touché." He removed both skillets, turned the burners off and scooped the bacon and a thick slab of French toast onto her plate, set it in front of her. "I'm just trying to ease the tension between them."

"I haven't detected any tension. And besides, Mac would have a say in any decision also."

"Pretend I never mentioned it."

He set his plate beside hers, came around the island and took his seat.

In silence, she scooped fresh peaches Marilyn had canned onto her toast while he drowned his in maple syrup.

"So what's up with you and Colson? Picking up where things left off?"

If only she could turn back the clock and do just

that. "That train pulled out of the station a long time ago. He has responsibilities and he'll be leaving when Mom and Dad come back."

"You really had it bad for him. And he hurt you. You shouldn't be stuck working with him."

"It was a long time ago. And it's only two more weeks now." But this had been the longest week of her life.

"Counting the days, huh?"

"Emmett." She rolled her eyes.

They stopped talking, the silence broken only by forks scraping plates.

"Where'd Colson get the kid?"

Resa looked out the window, to find Colson holding Cheyenne's hand as she skipped down the path to the barn. "That's his daughter, Cheyenne."

"Daughter?"

"Remember? He married Felicity Birmingham."

Emmett's sharp intake of breath drew her gaze to him.

"What?"

"Nothing. We ended up at the same college. She was too young to die." He stood, rounded the island. "I better get my things and jet." Dishes clattered as he set them in the sink.

"Hey, that's Grandma's china. Careful!" she called over her shoulder.

"Sorry." He bolted for the stairs.

Leaving her to frown after him, until the doorbell rang. She hurried to the foyer, then hesitated. Could it be Colson?

Colson Kincaid in her face every day. Oh, how had she let this happen? There had to be another foreman who could take over at a moment's notice.

Bracing herself, she opened the door.

There he stood, handsome as ever, and alone this time. He stepped inside and closed the door behind him. "Morning."

"Where's Cheyenne?" She looked behind him.

"At the barn with Annette. What about Emmett? Did he leave?" The foreboding in his tone tugged her gaze up to his. "I heard a car late last night."

What was it between Colson and Emmett? They were so wary of each other. "He's upstairs. He just made me the most wonderful French toast. Do you think Cheyenne might want some?"

"No!" Colson's jaw clenched. "I mean—she already ate." He shifted his weight from one foot to the other.

Did he not want Cheyenne around Emmett or something? Her brother certainly wasn't the most stand-up guy, but he wasn't a danger to children. Just companies.

"Has Mac ever mentioned my dad wanting to move our corporate offices or going public?"

"That was an abrupt subject change. No. But we don't really talk company business. Why?"

"Emmett mentioned it. Apparently Dad wants to move our headquarters to some upscale skyscraper in San Antonio and take our stock public." Which would irrevocably change the legacy of Rusticks. "But Mom doesn't." Surely Dad couldn't seriously want to go against everything his father had worked so hard to build.

"Let me guess whose side Emmett is on."

She speared Colson with a narrowed gaze.

"I'm just saying, Emmett's all about lining his own pockets. What do you think he's doing here, fixing you breakfast? I mean—it sounds like he's buttering you up or something."

"I won't stand here and listen to you trash—"

"I know he's your brother. But I wouldn't trust him if I were you."

"You're lecturing me about trust? I trusted you once and got third degree burns." Her chest squeezed as the words slipped out. Great! Now he knew how badly he'd broken her heart.

He winced. "I'm sorry. I just don't want you to get hurt. A woman in your position, heir of a vibrant company—it would pay you to be careful."

"Emmett may be reckless and irresponsible but he'd never hurt the company." Besides, he couldn't do anything without a majority vote. Could he? "Just get out."

"Out of your house or out of Bandera?"

"You're here because I need a ranch foreman, but stay out of my way. I don't need any advice from you."

"I'm out of here," Emmett called as he descended

the stairs. He stopped abruptly when he saw the two of them.

"I better get to work." Colson turned away, hurried outside. As if rabid coyotes nipped at his heels.

"What's up with y'all?" Resa set her hand on her hip and leveled a piercing gaze at her brother.

"Nothing." He shrugged. "I never liked him much. Guess the feeling's mutual." He came down the rest of the stairs, set his suitcase down. "Listen. I only want what's best for the company."

"Really? The company?" She crossed her arms under her chest, raised her chin. "Or what's best for your bank account?"

"This family means everything to me." His eyes turned glossy. "I've wasted years disappointing Mom and Dad. Letting them down. Letting you down. I'm trying to turn that around."

"Then stay here and help me while Mom and Dad are gone."

He closed his eyes. "You know rustic furniture has never been my thing. You live and breathe it. Just look at this place." He spread his arms wide, encompassing the whole of her house—log beams and furniture, suede fabrics, with horse-themed accents. "I'm more into sleek decor."

"Maybe we could start a new line."

He shook his head. "I'm not into designing furniture, period."

"Then what *are* you into?" A longing to connect with him welled up within her.

"Seriously?"

"Seriously."

"Video games. I created my own game. I'm meeting with a developer tomorrow."

"Really." She tried to infuse her voice and expression with enthusiasm. Not let it show that she thought him childish.

"I think it might really come together for me. One little game can put me on the map, and I can start my own company."

She might not be excited, but he was, and it was fulfilling to see his eyes light up. Even if she didn't understand him. And never would.

"I'm excited for you. Proud of you. Let me know how it goes."

"Thanks." His chest puffed up. "I will." He hugged her tight.

A remnant of the closeness they'd once shared.

"I better go." He let go of her, picked up his suitcase and headed for the door. Hand on the knob, he turned back to face her, a question in his eyes.

"What?"

"Nothing. Um, don't say anything to Mom and Dad about this. I don't want them disappointed again if nothing comes of it."

"I won't. But think positive."

"You were always the one to corner that market." He grinned, saluted her and exited.

Had Emmett finally decided to grow up? Maybe

there was hope for him yet. And she'd do everything she could to support him.

In the meantime, she had to deal with Colson. Even though she'd told him to stay out of her way, he couldn't really do that while he ran her ranch.

And now he knew she was still suffering from the broken heart he'd left her with.

Why had Ruby's mom wanted to pick her daughter up at Resa's office? Couldn't the woman have chosen somewhere else? Anywhere else? Colson pulled off his thick work gloves and opened the barn door—to find Cheyenne's head resting against Resa's arm as she worked on a blueprint. Their likeness almost stole his breath.

"Daddy!" Cheyenne lurched toward him.

"Better not get too close." He stepped inside, but made sure he stayed on the welcome mat. Even though he'd stomped his boots outside he was bound to drag in dirt. "I moved cattle today, so I'm extra filthy."

"I don't care, Daddy." Cheyenne hugged him for all she was worth. "I had so much fun with Ruby today. And her mama said I could come to their house sometime."

"We'll see." It was his standard response when he wasn't comfortable with an idea yet.

"Resa let me stay here and watch her work until you came. She said I can be a furniture designer like her when I grow up."

"She did, huh?"

Blue eyes clashed with his. "Her grandpa owns half the business." She shrugged. "I figure it's in her blood."

His sharp intake of breath startled Cheyenne.

She pulled away from him. "What's wrong, Daddy? Don't you want me to be a furniture designer?"

"You can be anything you want to be, princess."

"That's what Resa said."

He patted Cheyenne's head, but couldn't tug his gaze away from Resa.

"You might have had more fun with Annette for the last thirty minutes." He saw Resa make a few adjustments to the blueprint, then set her pencil down. "I hope I didn't bore you."

"I wasn't bored." Cheyenne darted back to her side. "Come see what she's drawing, Daddy. It's a log bunk bed with a foo…"

He stepped close enough to see. Close enough to get wrapped up in tropical perfume. "A futon."

"That's it. It has a futon on the bottom." Cheyenne tucked a strand of hair behind her ear that had slipped out of her braid. "That's a couch that slides down to make a bed."

"Cool."

"Here, Cheyenne, can you make this line a little darker for me?"

"Me?"

"I was about your age when my grandpa started letting me help him."

Cheyenne took the pencil she offered. Her teeth captured her bottom lip as she concentrated, darkening the line along the bunk-bed top as Resa instructed.

She was so good with the child. So wary with him. But that was probably a good thing. The last thing he needed was to let his heart get tangled up with his daughter's aunt.

"That's perfect." Resa hugged Cheyenne. "You're really good at this."

"Thanks."

"We better go, princess. I'm making my famous chili."

"You should come try it." Cheyenne's eyes widened. "It's really spicy."

Please, no.

"Thanks for the offer, but I have some things to do at my house."

"Anything I can do for you?" Colson asked.

"I can't think of a thing I need from you." She stood, turned away and grabbed her jacket.

It might be easier to keep her at bay while she was mad at him. But it didn't settle well.

Over the last ten days, he'd made headway with her. Seen a chink in her armor. A visible softening toward him. But their disagreement yesterday had picked the scabs off the wounds he'd inflicted on her.

If he could change one thing, leaving Resa behind would be it. But if their course had been different, he wouldn't have Cheyenne. Losing Resa again would hurt. But Cheyenne was worth every fragment of his crumbling heart.

Hunkered over the blueprint, Resa refused to risk a glance at the window. She should have closed her blinds when she got here this morning.

A knock sounded at the door.

Surely he wouldn't bother her, not after she'd told him to stay away from her.

She straightened, steeled herself just in case. "Come in."

Colson entered, leaned a hip against the massive log chair across from her desk. "I came to apologize for the other day and then I'm officially out of your way."

Stony silence. She liked being mad at him. Liked the prospect of him being out of her way.

"The whole Emmett thing is none of my business."

But she should accept his apology.

"You were trying to help." She set her pencil down, stretched her shoulders back. Something popped, then eased up. "I'm stressed out from worrying about the store and the ranch. And now I'm worried there might be trouble between my parents."

"If it makes you feel any better, I didn't see any

tension at the renewal ceremony. Just two very happy people deeply in love."

Her gaze met his. "Then why did Daddy change the date? You know, originally he had me book the dude ranch in March for their vow renewal. On their actual wedding anniversary. But then he switched it to December, on the date they met. You don't think he changed it because they were fighting about the store earlier in the year?"

"He told my dad he changed it because your mom would expect something in March." Colson sank into the chair, stirring up a leather scent along with his spicy cologne. "But not in December, and he wanted to really surprise her."

"That's what he told me, too."

"Not to make you mad again, but whose word do you trust more?" Colson's tone was gentle. "Emmett's or your dad's?"

"You're right."

"If you're so worried about this, why don't you phone your dad and discuss it with him?"

"I made him promise we wouldn't discuss business when they call." She propped her elbows on her desk, leaned her face into her hands.

"So how did they sound the last time you talked to them?"

She straightened again, with a smile tugging at her heart. "Blissful."

"There you go."

"I'm sorry for jumping all over you yesterday."

She drew in a shuddery breath. "You have every right to question Emmett's motives. He's manipulated me for years. I never know if I can trust him to not have some hidden agenda, so why should you?"

"I shouldn't have said anything." His attention turned to the window and he purposely strode over to it. "Oh no."

"What?"

"Peaches isn't in the barn lot."

"She looked ready to foal yesterday. Maybe she's in her stall." Resa jumped up, hurried to the door.

"No. The gate's open."

Her stomach sank. "She could be anywhere."

"I took Cheyenne in the lot yesterday to help with her fear, but I closed the gate. Should have checked it better."

"It's not your fault." Resa joined him at the window. No Peaches. "She's an expert gate opener, but I thought we were okay, since Juan installed a new latch. I should have put a backup on the catch. We have to find her before dark. If she has the foal, it might get too cold."

"I'm more concerned about coyotes getting to them." He dug his cell out and made a call. "Hey, Leon, I need all available hands searching for the palomino mare and possibly her foal. I'll take the south pasture." He paused. "That's right. Thanks."

Resa grabbed her jacket. "I'm going with you."

"Don't you have something to design?"

"The Christmas crunch is waning for me. I can spare a day. Especially for Peaches."

"Let's go."

So much for avoiding him. But Peaches and Cream were worth a day spent with Colson.

Chapter Ten

Saddle creaking with each movement his horse made, Colson tried to ignore the fog of tropical fruit wafting beside him. Cool air, leather and horse, yet Resa's perfume trumped everything. He searched the yellowed hills for anything stirring.

"She just has to be a palomino—the same color of dead grass and bare ground this time of year." Resa shielded her eyes from the sun. "I wish she'd come if you call her name, like a dog."

"Is she your horse?"

"Yes, as is her mother." Her gaze never left the rolling hills. "Her grandmother was Daddy's and he let me have her foal, Peaches's mom, Alabaster."

"You ride often?"

"Not as much as I'd like."

"It suits you. I don't know that I've ever seen you so relaxed, even with your horse missing."

"I think I see something."

His gaze followed hers.

"In that clearing on the second hill, I think something moved."

"Let's go." He swished the reins and his bay took off in a gallop.

Not one to follow, Resa soon passed him.

A few hundred yards closer, he could see the horse—standing, licking something.

"There's the foal!" Resa shouted over her shoulder.

Conversation ceased as they galloped toward the pair, the baby horse lying at its mother's feet.

"Good job, girl." Resa reined her horse at the bottom of the hill, swung down and approached the mare. "It's a girl. What a pretty baby." Peaches whinnied as Resa stroked her snout. "Can I pet her?"

The foal stood, spindly legs straining, as the mare whinnied again, then nudged Resa as if giving her approval.

Resa ran her palm along the foal's side. "Little Cream looks like she's just perfect."

"Keep her calm while I check them out." Colson climbed down from his saddle and approached.

With more soothing words, Resa stroked the mare and her foal.

"Peaches looks fine." Colson ran his hands along the foal's body, tested its legs. "And so does Cream. We just need to get them back to the barn, so they'll be warm and safe."

"Can Cream walk that far?"

"If you'll keep Peaches calm, I'll carry Cream on my horse."

"How will you get her up there?"

"Very carefully. See to the mama and I'll handle her foal."

"We're trying to help, Peaches." Resa stroked the horse's side. "I promise we won't hurt your baby."

Colson wrapped his arms under the foal's legs and picked her up. "Easy does it, little girl. I gotcha."

Peaches nickered in disapproval, stamped a foot.

"It's okay," Resa soothed, laying her cheek against the mare's muzzle. "We're just gonna get her back to the barn. You can come, too."

"We'll go nice and slow, 'cause she worked hard on this little project." Colson grasped the reins as he settled the foal across his horse, then held the little body steady as he mounted.

Resa swung up into her own saddle, clicked her tongue at the mare. "Come on, let's go home."

With the foal's warm body cradled against him, Colson urged his bay into a slow walk, then made the call to let the hands know they'd found Peaches and Cream.

The ride back seemed to take forever with a tired Peaches trailing behind them. Finally, they arrived at the barn.

"It's okay, girl." Resa dismounted, then smoothed her hand along Peaches's side as Colson carefully lifted the foal off his horse and set her in the stall.

With her baby safely on the ground, Peaches moved forward and nudged her with her nose.

"I'll make sure the gate is secure, install a second latch." Colson dumped grain in the trough, put the hose in the water barrel and turned it on.

"We should go get Cheyenne. Maybe she'll want to see Cream," Resa suggested. "With the foal so small, maybe she won't be afraid. Might even pet her."

"Not sure that's a good idea. Some mares get protective of their foals." He'd seen it happen and wouldn't take the chance with Cheyenne.

"Peaches isn't like that. Look how calm she's been with us. And this isn't her first."

"I guess you're right. But we should let them rest up for tonight." And give him time to think about it.

"Okay." Resa gave Peaches's hip a reassuring pat and backed out of the stall. "But I'm leaving for a weekend trade show tomorrow afternoon and I want Cheyenne to see Cream before I go."

"We'll see." Was he sad to see her go? Or glad? A mixture, he supposed. He'd miss her, but he was relieved for the reprieve.

"Thank you for taking care of Cream. I never could have gotten her up on my horse."

"Just doing my job." And trying his hardest not to let Resa's familiar, magnetic blue eyes undo him.

"We need to triple-lock the stall door, since we'll be gone to Bible study tonight."

"Wow, it is Wednesday."

"I assumed you were going. If not, Cheyenne could go with me."

"Wouldn't miss it." But he was rethinking his church choice. Surely there was somewhere else he and Cheyenne could go. Where Resa wasn't. But Marilyn had already charmed Cheyenne, and Ruby was there.

He'd just have to redouble his efforts to ignore Resa's presence.

Cloudless sky, bright morning sunshine, a nip in the December air. Resa stepped up on her parents' porch, her finger hesitating over the doorbell. She probably should have waited for Colson to come to the barn. But she had a jillion things to do before leaving today. And she wanted to witness Cheyenne's reaction when she saw the foal.

Seconds passed. She heard scurried, hurried footfalls, and then the door whooshed open.

"Resa!" Cheyenne zoomed into her.

Resa knelt, hugged the child. The perfect opportunity. Maybe she could bypass him, tell Mac their destination instead. But that wouldn't be right just because everything inside her longed to avoid Colson.

"Did your daddy tell you about Peaches's baby?"

"Uh-huh."

"Have you seen little Cream?"

"Not yet."

Heavy footfalls approached, then green eyes met hers. "We were just getting ready to head to the barn."

"Is it okay if I tag along?"

"Doesn't seem like I've got too much choice, since you're here."

Obviously, he wished she wasn't.

"Let's go, Daddy." Cheyenne grabbed his hand, then Resa's.

Resa stood. "Ready when y'all are."

"I'm taking Cheyenne to the barn," Colson hollered into the house.

"Okay, I'll come get her in a bit," Annette called.

Cheyenne darted out, but Colson stopped on the porch, his face close to Resa's. "You weren't planning to take her without me, were you?"

"Of course not." Not really. Sort of. Wishful thinking.

"I'll decide if she steps a toe in the barn lot. Got it?"

She couldn't explain that she'd only thought of going around him because she wanted to avoid him, because being near him made her long for the relationship they'd once had.

"What you say goes. You're her father."

His eyes dulled and he hurried down the steps. "Wait up, Cheyenne."

Resa followed and caught up with them. Cheyenne's little fingers sought hers again. Hand in hand, like a family, they headed to the barn, with Cheyenne skipping between the adults.

"Swing me."

On the count of three, they swung her high in

the air. Swinging and giggling punctuated the rest of their stroll.

At the barn, Cheyenne sobered with her first glimpse of Peaches, but a smile lit her face when she saw tiny Cream. "She's so little."

"She's just a baby." Colson picked Cheyenne up, leaned against the fence.

"Do you want to pet her?" Resa asked.

"Will her mommy mind?"

"Peaches is really gentle and proud of her little girl. She won't mind at all."

Cheyenne stretched her arms toward Resa. "Can you take me?"

Something in Colson's eyes died.

"I think your daddy wants to do that."

"It's all right." His tone grave, he handed Cheyenne to her. "Take her. I'll go in first."

He was obviously still worried Peaches might develop a protective streak as long as his own.

Cheyenne's arms clamped around Resa's neck, her knees around her hips, as Colson opened the gate to the barn lot for them.

"Hey, Peaches, Cheyenne wants to see your pretty little baby." Resa strolled toward the mare and her foal.

"Her legs are so long." Cheyenne chuckled. "She looks like a baby deer."

"You're right." Resa patted Peaches's shoulder as they reached her. Cream stretched her spindly legs when Resa knelt, and Cheyenne tentatively laid her hand on the baby's back.

"She's so soft."

"Her coat's all fresh and clean."

Peaches nuzzled Cheyenne's arm and the little girl sucked in a big breath, raised up and pressed her cheek against Resa's shoulder.

"It's okay. She just wants some attention, too. You know where her favorite place to be petted is?"

"Where?"

"Just between her nostrils." Resa stroked Peaches's snout. "You wanna try?"

With a slow nod, Cheyenne tentatively stuck her hand out.

Resa leaned until she could reach Peaches.

"It's soft, too." Cheyenne's voice filled with wonder.

"Like velvet."

"She's so sweet." Cheyenne giggled as Peaches nuzzled her hand.

"Maybe you can ride her some day."

"Maybe." But Cheyenne didn't sound so sure.

Resa's phone rang. "Sorry, sweet pea, but this is work." She gave Peaches a final pat and turned toward the barn, digging her phone from her pocket. It was her floor manager. Colson got the gate for her, then took Cheyenne and set her down.

"Hey, Nina."

"I tried to cancel the extra hotel room for tonight,

but it's too late. Either way, we have to pay for it. So I thought you might want to invite a friend."

"Thanks for trying."

"Other than that, everything's taken care of. I confirmed our reservations. The hotel is right on the beach and twenty-eight minutes from the convention center."

"What would I do without you?" Resa propped her foot on the fence railing, watched Peaches nuzzle Cream.

"Work more than you already do." Nina chuckled. "Please promise me we'll at least enjoy the beach while we're there."

"Feel free to enjoy the beach during our stay, but I'm pretty sure I won't have time."

"Make time. I'm fixing to head out, so I can oversee our display setup. And Ginger is handling the store."

"Thanks. I'll check in with you before I leave this afternoon." She ended the call, tucked her phone back in her pocket.

"Are you going to the beach, Resa?" Cheyenne's eyes were wide and dreamy.

"I have a trade show in Corpus Christi. It's where furniture stores set up in a huge convention center and show off what we make."

"Can I come, too?"

"Cheyenne," Colson scolded. "We don't invite ourselves along."

"I'm sorry, Daddy." Cheyenne pouted.

"You like the beach, sweet pea?" Resa asked.

"I love it. We used to go there a lot."

"Kingsville is near Corpus." Colson stroked Cheyenne's braid. "We'll go again soon."

"I'd love to take her with me. Annette could come, too, so when I have to work, they could play on the beach. And we have an extra hotel room, since one of our salesmen had to cancel."

"Can I, Daddy? Can I?"

"You're not going anywhere without me, sweetheart."

"Then you come, too, Daddy."

Resa almost swallowed her tongue. "Sure, you both could come." She wouldn't mind Cheyenne and Annette coming along. But not Colson. Surely he wouldn't agree. "But your daddy may not be able to get away from the ranch."

"But Daddy bought all the cattle and Mr. Leon is here. Daddy just tells Mr. Leon what to do, so he could do that before he leaves."

Colson gave a sheepish look. "I do a bit more than that."

Resa laughed. "Sounds like Mr. Leon might need a raise."

"Please, Daddy. It's been forever since we've gone to the beach."

"Only if Resa is okay with me leaving Leon in charge, and if she'll let me pay for the room."

"Please, Resa."

She was out of excuses. "Leon can handle things

here. But you don't have to pay—the room is yours if you want it." She held her breath.

"I insist on paying. We better pack your bags, princess."

"Yay!" Cheyenne hugged his neck.

"Resa will be working, so we may not even see her during our stay."

"But we can ride together all the way there. And all the way back home. Right?"

It just kept getting worse.

"Resa will need her car while she's there."

A reprieve.

"Oh." Cheyenne frowned. "But whoever called is going, too. Right?"

"My floor manager, Nina, is leaving soon." It really didn't make sense for Colson and Resa to both make the drive this afternoon.

"You can ride with us, then with her for work stuff once you get there, right?" Cheyenne looked so hopeful.

At past trade shows, she and other employees had done exactly that.

"It's settled then. What time do we need to leave?" Colson asked.

"About one, so we can miss rush hour. Be sure and tell Leon to keep a close watch on Peaches and Cream."

"Will do." He checked his watch. "We'll be ready."

Once they got there, they'd go their separate

ways. Running into Cheyenne, borrowing her for some beach fun in the evenings, would be nice. But Resa would not spend the weekend with Colson.

"You sure you'll be all right back there?" Colson caught Resa's gaze in his rearview mirror.

"I'm fine." She smiled toward Cheyenne, who was beside her. "I want to sit with this one."

"You let me know if you start feeling bad."

"Are you sick, Resa?"

"No, sweet pea. I just get carsick sometimes, especially if I sit in the back. But I took a pill that helps with it. So I should be fine."

"Sometimes I get carsick, too. I'm not big enough to sit in the front yet. But Daddy says I will be someday soon." Cheyenne chattered about everything from Disney princesses to her favorite nail polish for the next several miles, then fell silent.

"Did you decide to let Resa get a word in?"

No response.

"Cheyenne, are you okay?" A tinge of worry rang in Resa's voice.

He adjusted his mirror so he could see her. His little girl was pale.

"Cheyenne? Are you all right?"

She met his gaze with a slight shake of her head.

"I'm pulling over at this gas station. Just hang on."

Cheyenne didn't say a word. Her eyes were huge, staring at Resa.

He pulled into the gas station. They'd barely stopped rolling when Resa bailed, zipped around the car and helped Cheyenne out.

His daughter lost it, just outside the car, then started to cry. "I made a mess."

"It's okay, sweet pea." Resa knelt to comfort her, oblivious of the puddle. "You didn't mean to."

A gray-haired woman exited the store. "Oh my."

Cheyenne pulled away from Resa, her cheeks going redder. "I got carsick."

"Don't you worry." The older woman winked at Cheyenne. "Your mama will take good care of you."

Resa gasped. "Oh no, I'm not her mom."

"Really? Well, she's the spitting image of you."

A steel band closed around Colson's chest. "Their coloring is similar, huh?"

"I want her to be my mommy." Cheyenne sounded sad.

"Well, I hope you get your wish." The woman climbed into her car, then waved as she backed up.

"Let's go in the bathroom." Resa stood. "We'll wash your face and I always keep a spare toothbrush in my purse. That'll make you feel better."

"Okay." Cheyenne clasped her hand.

Inside the store, they searched out the ladies' room. Hand in hand, Resa and Cheyenne disappeared inside. For once, Colson was glad Resa was with them. He couldn't have gone in with Cheyenne to help her clean up. And he hated taking her to the men's room.

Cheyenne was right. She needed a mom. But Resa was her aunt. And he couldn't let them discover the truth. Yet a complete stranger had seen it—a close call.

He strolled to the counter. "My daughter had a little accident in your parking lot."

"I saw." The kind-eyed man at the register winced. "Poor thing."

"Carsick. Is there a water hose I could clean it up with?"

"Don't worry. My son will take care of it. He broke curfew last night and I've been trying to come up with the perfect punishment."

"You're welcome?" Colson managed a smile.

Minutes later, the door opened. Cheyenne came out, looking not as pale or as sad.

"There we go." Resa pressed a wet cloth to one cheek, then the other, then across her forehead.

"Oh, that feels good."

"Maybe we should just sit outside for a bit. Fresh air usually helps."

Colson opened the door for them, then took Cheyenne's free hand and cut around the side of the store.

"We'll just sit here until you feel okay." Resa plopped down on the curb, pulled Cheyenne into her lap. "Take as long as you need."

"I'm tired."

"Maybe you can sleep the rest of the drive."

"Come sit with us, Daddy."

He settled beside Resa. Despite the good foot of space he kept between them, he could feel her nearness. Smell her perfume. He should have never let Cheyenne talk him into this trip. Once they arrived at Corpus, he and Cheyenne needed to avoid her. Not see each other again, until Sunday afternoon for the trip home.

"I'm sorry I didn't realize she was feeling ill. I should have been watching her. But I was looking at the road so I wouldn't get sick myself."

"It's not your fault. I should have fed her a lighter breakfast. I should know by now she doesn't travel very far on a full stomach."

"I think she's asleep."

Colson leaned forward to get a glimpse of Cheyenne's face. "She is. Poor baby, she'll probably sleep the rest of the way. Let me take her."

"I'm fine, if you can help me up." With her arm around Cheyenne, Resa reached her hand toward him.

"You won't be able to get her high enough to reach her car seat in the truck."

"I guess you're right. I think she weighs twice as much when she's asleep."

"I know, trust me." He stood, scooped Cheyenne into his arms. "I've got her."

They strolled to the vehicle and Resa opened the door, then situated the belt on the car seat. Cheyenne barely stirred as he settled her in place and strapped her in. By the time he shut the door, Resa was buckling her seat belt beside Cheyenne in the back.

"Look. I'm sorry we crashed your trip," he said as he climbed in. "I got excited because Cheyenne was raring to go the beach. It's been a long time since she's been enthusiastic about anything."

"You didn't crash my trip. She's an absolute doll and I want her to have fun. In fact, I don't know what I'll do when y'all leave."

His gaze collided with hers in the rearview mirror.

"I mean—I'll miss Cheyenne."

He started the engine. Resa and Cheyenne were getting way too close. Which meant she was getting way too close to discovering the truth. He could lose his little girl…the way he was losing his heart to Resa all over again.

Chapter Eleven

Her feet aching, her shoulders stiff and her back sore, Resa got in the elevator after a long day on the convention floor. As the door started to slide closed, she heard a pair of rushing feet.

"Hold, please." It was Colson, carrying a droopy-eyed Cheyenne.

She stopped the door.

"Resa!" Cheyenne roused as her dad stepped in.

"Thanks. How'd it go today?" he asked.

"Lots of orders from the spring and summer lines." She hadn't seen them since they'd checked in yesterday afternoon, even though their room was right across the hall. "Somebody looks sleepy."

"Will you tuck me in?"

Like a mother. The last thing she wanted to do. And yet the thing she wanted to do most. "If your daddy doesn't mind."

"Resa might be too tired."

"I'm fine." Why hadn't she taken the out he offered?

The elevator stopped several times, more people getting on and off, and they fell into silence.

"I'm tired, Daddy." Cheyenne yawned again.

"I know, princess. We're almost there."

The elevator stopped on their floor and they exited.

Maybe Cheyenne was already asleep, which would let her off the hook.

They reached their rooms and Cheyenne's little head popped up. "You're still tucking me in, right, Resa?"

"Of course."

Colson unlocked the door and she followed him inside. The suite was much like hers.

"The bedroom's through here." He ushered her ahead of him.

Two queen beds, as opposed to her single king.

He set Cheyenne on one of them. "Let me get your pajamas." He dug in a pink suitcase.

"I can get her changed."

"Okay." Disappointment echoed clear in his voice. He handed over a pink flannel nightgown decorated with princesses, and stepped back into the living room, closing the door behind him.

Minutes later, Cheyenne was tucked in, already sound asleep. Resa eased the door open, closed it silently. Colson sat on the couch.

"She asleep already?"

"Pretty much fell asleep sitting up."

"It was a big day for her. For you, too. Thanks for taking time to tuck her in, even though you're dead on your feet." He patted the cushion beside him. "Have a seat."

"I enjoyed it." She sank onto the couch, careful to keep a good two feet of space between them.

"You're good with her. Felicity was always awkward around her. Didn't spend much time with her daughter at all."

Resa's heart clenched. How could a mother be awkward around her child?

"It's like they never bonded. I tried to make up for it by lavishing her with affection. But little girls need their mommies."

"You've done a great job with her. Does she remember much about Felicity?"

"I don't think so." He leaned back, propped his feet on the coffee table. "Probably a good thing. We argued a lot."

"I'm sorry."

"Me, too." He leaned his head back, stared at the ceiling, as if he'd somehow find the answers there. "We never got along. Before Cheyenne, we'd fight, break up, get together again. I don't know why we didn't go our separate ways. I guess you figured out Cheyenne was the only reason I married her."

"It didn't get better after she was born?"

"She cheated on me. More than once."

"I'm so sorry. I had no idea you were so miserable." He'd done the right thing. Giving Cheyenne his name. Supporting them. Yet Felicity hadn't appreciated his effort. Had she known about Resa? That he'd sacrificed their future to do right by Felicity?

"After Felicity and my mom, I've given up on trusting women." He closed his eyes. "No offense. Cheyenne is the one bright spot. It was worth it, since I got her out of the relationship."

He let out a heavy breath. "Felicity couldn't help the way she was. Her mom was cold toward her, let the nanny raise her. Her dad tried to make up for it, and spoiled her terribly. She could never see past what she wanted, as if no one else mattered in her world. I hope I'm not following their pattern with Cheyenne."

"You're not. You're a great dad and I don't see any sign of you spoiling her."

"I try." His vulnerability tugged at Resa.

She yawned. "I better get to my room, before I fall asleep sitting here."

He stood, followed her to the door. "Maybe we'll see you tomorrow."

"Maybe." More than anything, she wanted to hug him. To feel his arms around her. Give him comfort. Instead, she turned to the door, tugged it open and bolted across the hall to her room. Her longing to get away from him warred with her longing to get closer to him.

It had been a long day, much of it filled once again with thoughts of father and daughter. Why did she miss them? Not him, just Cheyenne. *Yeah, right.*

As Resa slid in her key card, the door across the hall behind her opened. She squeezed her eyes shut, both eager for and dreading the sight of him.

"Resa!"

She turned, just in time to catch Cheyenne as she hurled herself into her legs. "Hey, sweet pea. Did you play on the beach today?"

"Me and Daddy built a huge sand castle and we picked up little bitty shells." She dug in her pocket, pulled out a handful of treasures. "It was weird. The water would rush in and the shells wash up, but some of them sucked down into the sand. Daddy said there were little sea creatures living in them. But I picked up empty shells."

"They're beautiful." Resa knelt to eye level with the child, but chanced a glance at Colson. He was leaning against the door to their room, hands stuffed in his pockets.

"Are you done working for the day?" The hopeful lilt in Cheyenne's tone turned Resa's insides to jelly.

"Yes. But I'm so tired."

"Oh." Cheyenne's bottom lip stuck out in a sulk. "I was hoping you'd come to supper with us. We're going to Snoopy's Pier."

"I love seafood. But I was planning to order room service." In her jammies. And eat in bed.

"But we won't make you run or nothing. You'll just get to sit there and eat."

Resa chuckled.

"Don't bother Resa, princess. Let's go so she can get some rest."

"She's not bothering me." Resa's gaze dueled it out with his.

"Then you'll come with us?" Cheyenne prompted.

"I'd love to."

"Yay!" Cheyenne clapped her hands. "Let's go."

"Can you give me a minute? Let me freshen up."

"You don't need to. You're beautiful."

"Thank you, sweet pea, but—"

"Isn't she beautiful, Daddy?"

Colson cleared his throat. "Uh, yeah. But I think Resa might want to grab her flip-flops. She'd have a hard time walking the beach in her heels and skirt."

"I doubt there'll be much beach walking, since it's dark, but my feet *are* killing me. Tell you what, y'all go down to the lobby and I'll meet you there in just a few minutes."

"Okay." Cheyenne took Colson's hand and they headed for the elevator.

Resa opened her door, stepped inside, leaned her back against the wall and kicked her shoes off. How had she ended up agreeing to dinner with them? While she was falling in love with his daughter, it seemed Colson had also finagled his way into her heart again. How had she let it happen?

"Yum." Cheyenne's fish and chips were half-gone.

Once their food arrived, things had gone quiet.

For the first time, Colson noticed the chatter among other diners.

Resa had barely said a word. He glanced at her, then away, out the window beside their table overlooking the beach. There was just a sliver of moon, but the restaurant lighting cast a glow over the shore. Enough to see movement below.

"Look at the ghost crabs." Colson pointed with his fork.

"Why are they ghosts, Daddy?"

"They're not, and I told you, there's no such thing as ghosts. They just call them that because they're the same color as the sand and it makes it hard to see them."

"Oh. Do they pinch people?"

"Maybe if you try to pick them up or accidentally step on them."

"Were they on the beach when we were there today, Daddy?"

"No, princess. They mostly come out at night to eat."

"I don't wanna walk the beach at night then."

"It's probably too cool, anyway."

The clatter of silverware drew his gaze back to Resa.

Her blue eyes large, she swallowed hard, and Colson suddenly noticed splotches all over her neck.

"Resa, you're all spotted." Cheyenne frowned. "Are you all right?"

"I think I'm having—" she gasped "—an allergic reaction." She dug in her purse.

"What can I do?" He got up, went to her side.

She pulled something out of her purse, jammed it into her outer thigh, held it there for several seconds. "EpiPen."

"Should I call 911?"

"I don't think so."

He grabbed his phone, jabbed in the numbers, ready to hit Send.

"I think I'll be okay. Maybe outside. I need some air."

"Check, please."

Big tears rolled down Cheyenne's face. He pulled her into his lap.

"I'll be okay." Resa managed a tremulous smile. "Don't worry."

Her breathing seemed to have eased, but her lips looked swollen.

The waiter's eyes went wide when he brought their ticket. "Ma'am, are you all right? Are you allergic to fish? Or shellfish?"

"I've eaten it—" she sucked in air "—my whole life."

"Dr. Stan, over here," the waiter urged.

A silver-haired man got up from a table on the other side, rushed toward them.

"See, there's a doctor here." Colson moved out of the way back to his side of the table, rocked

Cheyenne, wiped her cheeks. "He'll make sure Resa is okay."

"Please." Resa pressed a hand against her throat. "I'm fine."

"Are you allergic to anything?" The doctor settled beside Resa, took her wrist, checked his watch. "Is this your plate? Fish, shrimp, crab?"

"Yes. I'm allergic to bees. I already used my EpiPen."

"Did you get stung?"

"No."

"Any fish or shellfish allergies?"

"No."

"Until now."

"But I've eaten seafood my entire life."

"Shellfish allergies are known to develop well into adulthood."

"So I can't eat shrimp or crab anymore?" Resa sounded as if her life might be over.

"Not unless you like feeling like this."

"My face feels funny." She pressed a hand to her mouth and her eyes widened. "Are my lips swollen?"

"Just a little."

"Actually, a lot. You look kind of like Daffy Duck." Cheyenne giggled.

Resa laughed.

At least Cheyenne wasn't scared anymore, but Colson needed to talk to her about not hurting feelings with her honesty.

"Do you have another EpiPen—just in case?" the doctor asked.

"Yes."

He turned to Colson. "Take her to the ER to make sure her symptoms don't return."

"I will."

"Good." He patted Resa's arm. "After the ER, rest. Get some fresh air. Take Benadryl. Use cold compresses. Avoid hot showers and the sun."

"Thank you." Colson stood, shook the man's hand.

"Don't you worry, little darling, your mommy will be just fine." The doctor gave Cheyenne a reassuring smile and returned to his table.

"See?" Cheyenne looked up at him, all innocent. "Everybody thinks Resa is my mommy. So you should marry her, Daddy."

Resa scrambled to her feet. "I need air." She fled for the exit as the waiter brought the receipt.

Colson scribbled his name. "Young lady, stop with the mommy stuff."

"But I want Resa to be my new mommy."

"Trust me, I realize that. But Resa is sick. She doesn't need anything else making her uncomfortable. And we don't have that kind of relationship, anyway. Right now, can you focus on helping Resa feel better?"

"Yes, Daddy." Cheyenne's gaze dropped to the floor.

He scooped her up and hurried after Resa.

* * *

Resa opened her bedroom door.

Colson was sprawled on her couch, Cheyenne asleep on the love seat.

"What are you doing here?"

"Morning." He sat up. "How do you feel?"

"Fuzzy."

"You're rocking the Angelina Jolie look."

Her hand went to her mouth. "Or Donald Duck." She glanced at Cheyenne, who hadn't even stirred since they started talking. "You stayed here last night?"

"Cheyenne was worried about you. Let me get you some coffee." He stood, strode to the kitchen.

"I can't even describe how awesome that sounds." She followed and sank into a chair.

"Knocked the stuffing out of you, huh?"

"I called Nina when I woke up. Thanks for letting her know why I was a no-show for packing up this morning."

"No worries. Still three creamers, three sugars?"

"Yep. A little coffee with my cream and sugar."

He handed her a steaming mug.

"At least I've still got coffee." She moaned. "No seafood ever again."

"Sorry about that."

"I don't remember anything after leaving the hospital."

"You zonked out as soon as we hit the road. I

had to carry you in. Thankfully, Cheyenne stayed awake until we got to your room."

Carried her in? Her cheeks steamed. Safe and protected in Colson's arms. Right where she wanted to be. Right where she couldn't be. "Poor child. I ruined her supper."

"She was fine once you were."

Memories whirled. The doctor calling her Cheyenne's mommy. Cheyenne's challenge for them to make it so. Resa's face heated, causing her cheeks to itch.

"I need a cool shower. I still feel itchy." She stood, cradled her mug in both hands.

"Maybe after Cheyenne wakes up, we could go stroll the beach before we head out. You've worked so much, you never got to do that."

"Maybe." Or she could hide in her room. Avoid him as she'd planned, until it was time to load up his truck.

"What time do you want to leave?"

"I'd like to make it home in time for evening services, since I missed this morning."

"We'll be packed and ready."

She stopped, turned to face him. "I'm glad y'all were here. I'd have been all alone in the restaurant last night and ended up in an ambulance."

"Actually, you'd have ordered room service and not gotten sick. I'm just glad you're okay."

This afternoon, they'd make the three-hour drive

home. Then maybe things would get back to normal. And she might get her heart under control.

Yet deep down, she wished they didn't have to leave. That they could stay here forever and enjoy idyllic days on the beach together.

Chapter Twelve

The bedroom door opened. Resa emerged looking fresh. Wearing long shorts, a royal blue T-shirt, light sweater and flip-flops, she walked toward them, causing Colson's stomach to flip.

"Resa." Cheyenne darted toward her, then stopped. After a furtive glance toward Colson, she closed the gap between them slowly and gave her a gentle hug.

At least she'd remembered his caution about Resa being weak.

"I won't break. You can hug me better than that."

"Daddy said you're weak and itchy."

"The shower helped the itchy, but I am kind of puny."

"Can we go to the beach now?"

"Resa might not be up for that." The instinct to cradle her in his arms, protect her, welled within Colson. "You hungry?"

"I'm starving." Resa clasped a hand to her empty stomach.

"We could go back to Snoopy's Pier, since we didn't get to finish eating last night." Cheyenne's eyes widened and she clamped a hand over her mouth. "Sorry."

"It's okay, sweet pea. There's still lots of other things I can eat."

"We could have a picnic on the beach." Cheyenne cast hopeful eyes on Resa.

"I can't think of anything better. But my stomach may not be up to food just yet."

"The water's too cold, but we can pick up shells!" Cheyenne gave her usual little bounce.

"And then you can take a nap."

"I'm not sure I can stay out that long, though. The sun might make me itchy."

"But we have one of those huge umbrellas. It's in our room."

"We'll see how it goes."

"Come on." Cheyenne grabbed Resa's hand, jumped up and down.

"Don't rush her, princess."

"I'm fine." Resa smiled. "Let's go."

She was obviously enamored with his child. *With her niece.*

Colson gathered the blanket and umbrella and they made their way to the elevator. Other travelers—a few businessmen, a couple and a boisterous family—surrounded them. Several smiles were sent their way, as if they were a cute family.

The long walk to the beach seemed to tire Resa. He spread the blanket well away from the damp sand and set up the umbrella.

"Everything okay with the trade show?"

"Fine. We made lots of sales, took a boatload of orders. Nina and the crew loaded all the leftovers in the truck."

"Come wade with me, Resa." Cheyenne wiggled her toes in the sand.

"Let me sit here a minute." She sank to the blanket, in the shade of the umbrella.

"I think Resa might need to rest after all that walking." Colson tugged his daughter toward the beach. "I'll wade with you."

"Okay." She smiled up at him, as if he was still the center of her world.

"You sure you're okay?" he called to Resa.

"It's wonderful to be outside. Go on, I'll be right here."

He and Cheyenne ran toward the water, staying a few feet away from the wet sand. Her squeal as the tide rushed toward them warmed his heart. More squealing sounded as, hand in hand, they ran along the shore as the waves rolled in and out.

After several hundred yards, they turned around and went back the way they'd come. Cheyenne picked up a few shells, put them in the plastic bag he'd brought along.

"Did you see that, Daddy?"

"What?"

"That shell just sucked down in the sand."

"I want to see." Resa joined them.

Cheyenne clasped her hand. "Watch the shells on the beach real close when the tide rolls out."

The water rushed out and, sure enough, several shells were sucked down into the sand.

"Cool." Resa knelt to pick up one that stayed still.

But Colson grabbed her hand. "In light of what happened last night, do you think you should touch them."

"I hadn't even thought of it." Her gaze dropped to his hand, still holding hers.

He let go, picked up the shell for her and stashed it in Cheyenne's bag.

"I bet if we go way over there—" Resa pointed "—where there are fewer people, we could find more shells."

Colson scanned the beach peppered with tourists, then the expanse of unoccupied sand in the distance. "That's quite a way off. Are you sure you're up to it?"

"If we go slow." Resa shielded her eyes from the sun. "I'm having the time of my life. It's not every day I get to help Cheyenne find shells."

"If you get tired, we'll rest. And I can carry you back if I need to." His heart pinged. He certainly wouldn't mind having her in his arms again. "And we'll take the umbrella." He went and dug it out of the sand, then held it over her as they strolled along.

"I have a shell book at home." Resa scanned the horizon.

"A shell book?" The wonder in Cheyenne's words was infectious.

"It has pictures of all different kinds of shells and tells what kind they are, what kinds of creatures live in them, where to find them and how to tell them apart."

"Wow."

"When we get back to the ranch, we'll use it to see what kind of shells we've gathered."

"Where did you get it? Your book?"

"My mom got it for me. I've always loved seashells."

"Have you been here before?"

"Once. My family always visited Surfside Beach on vacation. It's close to Galveston. I have a whole shell collection from there. I'll let you see it if you want."

"Wow."

As the bond between them strengthened, Colson was powerless to stop it. Everything in him wanted to grab Cheyenne up and flee. But he couldn't. He was stuck at the ranch for another week. Helplessly watching Cheyenne bond with her aunt. With guilt eating at him for keeping them in the dark.

After a long first day back at his home-away-from-home, Colson headed to the house. He'd survived watching over Resa following the shellfish incident, the day at the beach spent with her, the drive home. He'd sat near her at evening services last night, then managed to avoid her all day today.

Two weeks down, one to go.

He stepped inside the mudroom, pulled off his boots and jacket.

"Daddy!" Cheyenne ambushed him.

He scooped her up, swung her around. "How was your day, princess?"

"Resa brought her shell book over. We're 'dentifying shells we picked up at the beach."

"Did you bother her about it?"

"Not really." She ducked her head. "Nette took me to see Peaches and Cream just as Resa was leaving her office, and I asked if I could borrow her book. She offered to bring it over."

"Okay." He steeled his spine, tried to erect a cage around his heart.

In the great room, Resa sat on the floor, ankles crossed in front of her. A huge drop cloth covered with piles of shells surrounded her. Annette and Dad were watching from the couch.

"Should you touch those?" Colson asked Resa.

"I checked with my doctor. He said it's fine as long as they've been cleaned. Annette soaked them in vinegar for me."

"I can help Cheyenne, if you need to go." *Please do.*

"I'm finished for the day, so I brought some of my own collection over."

She looked up at him and her blue eyes almost stole his breath.

"How you feeling?"

"Much better."

"That's good. Glad you're recovering." He'd shared insight into his marriage and told her he could never trust another woman, as a deterrent. Something, anything to keep her at bay. Before his traitorous heart fully embraced her. But it was obviously too late.

"What's this one?"

"That's a spotted slipper limpet."

"And this one."

"Hmm." Resa carefully took the shell from Cheyenne. "I'm not sure. Let's see if we can find it in the book."

Heads bent, scanning the pictures, the two looked so much alike. Cheyenne was a mirror image of what Resa must have looked like at that age. She looked and acted more like Cheyenne's mother than Felicity ever had. *If only she could be.*

Guilt and longing twisted like a knife in his gut.

"How about some lemonade?" Annette stood. "I'm thirsty."

"Yes, please." Cheyenne never looked up from the book.

But Resa did. "I can help."

"You stay put. Colson will help me."

Grateful for the escape, he trailed her into the kitchen.

"What's going on with y'all?" Annette looked up at him with a knowing grin.

"Nothing." So much for escape. He dug a tray from the cabinet, set it on the kitchen island.

"Don't give me that. Your father told me y'all were once a thing."

"A long time ago." He filled the glasses with ice, hoping the clink and clatter would deter her.

She got the pitcher from the fridge, began filling glasses, but as soon as the ice dispenser stopped, she was on him again. "There's still something there."

"She's my boss. That's all."

"Cheyenne told me about Resa's allergic reaction and how worried you were."

"I was worried about Cheyenne witnessing the whole thing."

Annette set the pitcher down. "Listen, I've never really tried to mother you, but I have some experience in this area. After my first husband left me, I didn't want anything to do with men. For years. But after a while, I was lonely." She traced the condensation on a glass with her finger.

"My daughter was still small when I finally dipped my toes back into the dating pool, but none of the men I met were interested in a package deal. Olivia was my priority, so I gave up, focused on my child until she was grown."

"And then you met Dad." Colson set the glasses on the tray. "Who would have loved her when she was young. I could have used your nurturing, too. I've often wondered why y'all didn't meet sooner."

"Me, too, but it's all in God's timing. Not ours. My point is, you don't have to search for someone to love—who could love Cheyenne. You've already found Resa."

"Whoa. I didn't say anything about love."

"Your eyes do when you look at her." Annette leaned a hip against the island. "What's holding you back?"

She was on to him. But he couldn't tell her the truth. That he was holding on to Cheyenne and his secret, that he had no claim on her.

"You can tell me. I won't say a word. Not even to your dad."

But he could tell her the rest of it. "Felicity's life was cut short because of me. I don't deserve to be happy."

"Oh, Colson. It was an accident."

"Was it?" Guilt and shame battled it out, tightening the band of pressure in his chest. "She hurt me so many times. Made my life miserable. Was working on making Cheyenne miserable. I can't help wondering if deep down, subconsciously, I knew the horse wasn't ready to be ridden. Maybe I set her up."

"That's the most ridiculous thing I've ever heard. You don't have it in you to hurt anyone. Not even if they hurt you first."

"Are you sure?"

"Positive." She reached across the island, gave

his hand a squeeze. "You have to let this go. Stop blaming yourself."

"Even if Felicity's death was an accident, I've made so many mistakes." Like intentionally withholding the truth from Resa and her parents.

"When you asked Jesus to be your savior, God forgot any past sins, and He's abundantly merciful toward future ones. He doesn't keep score on your wrongs. You do. You have to give that to Him. Let Him wipe your slate clean in your heart."

"I'll try." But what about intentionally withholding a truth to protect Cheyenne, to protect himself from losing her, but at the same time hurting the McCalls?

"You do that. And don't let Resa get away a second time." The older woman patted his arm before heading back to the great room. "I'll get the door for you."

Could his heart take losing Resa again? It didn't matter. He had no choice. Even if he embraced the notion that he was free to love again, Resa would have nothing to do with him if she knew the truth.

This had to stop. Spending time with Cheyenne meant Resa was spending too much time with Colson. She shouldn't have taken her shell book over last night. The little girl was blossoming. She didn't need Resa. She'd be leaving for Kingsville in just over a week. It would be better for both of them if they weaned themselves of the attachment now.

And Resa didn't need to pine over Colson when he left. Again. She had to stay away from him.

She'd worked all day, with her blinds pulled. No distractions, focused on designing. There weren't many orders in the lull before Christmas, but she hadn't come up with a single idea for something new for the showroom.

A tentative knock sounded at the barn door.

She frowned. "Come in."

"Sorry to bother you." Colson stuck his head in.

The exact reason she'd pulled her blinds.

"Cheyenne wants to ride Peaches. With you. Are you still open to riding double with her? I know you're trying to work, but she's ready now. And I'm afraid if she doesn't ride, she'll never be ready again. She insists she'll only ride with you."

Despite her misgivings, Resa couldn't say no to that request. "I'm actually done for the day." She set her pencil down. Done with nothing. "Be right with you."

"Thanks." He closed the door.

She slipped her cell in her pocket and grabbed her jacket. Tried to calm her heartbeat.

As she stepped outside, Cheyenne's excitement was palpable. "I'm gonna do it, Resa. I'm gonna ride."

"I'm so proud of you."

"I'll get a saddle." Colson disappeared inside the barn.

Cheyenne couldn't take her eyes off the mare. "When will Cream be old enough to ride?"

"When she's about two."

"Maybe Daddy can train her."

"Probably not, sweet pea." Resa rubbed circles on Cheyenne's back. "By then, you and your daddy will be back in Kingsville."

"I don't wanna go back. I wanna stay here with you." The little girl's plaintive tone tugged at her.

"Maybe you can come visit me." *Without your father.*

"Thanks for all the shells you gave me. After I ride Peaches, can you come to the house with your book again and sort some more?"

"I'm sorry, sweet pea. I've got things to do." *Like avoid your daddy.* "But you can borrow my book."

"Okay." Cheyenne wilted.

Colson came out of the barn with a saddle propped on his shoulder. Hand in hand, Resa and Cheyenne followed him into the barn lot. He nudged Cream to one side, set the blanket in place, lifted the saddle onto Peaches's back, fastened it, then tested it thoroughly.

"All set here."

Resa held the reins as she swung up into the saddle, then scooted back to make room for Cheyenne. The smell and creak of leather always warmed her insides.

"You ready?" Colson slipped his hands under Cheyenne's arms.

She nodded.

He picked her up. "Swing your leg over."

"This will be so much fun." Resa helped balance her slight weight. "Once you ride, you'll never want to stop."

"Keep it slow," Colson murmured.

"We have to, for Cream's sake. She'll go everywhere we do."

"I wish I could ride her." Cheyenne's voice quivered. "It wouldn't be as far down."

"You can get off if you want." Resa slipped her left arm around Cheyenne's middle. "But I won't let you fall. I promise."

"I want to ride."

"Hold on tight to the saddle horn." Colson patted her leg, but his eyes reflected his worry.

"I am, Daddy."

"We'll be fine. We'll just go around the lot once."

He removed his hand and Resa clicked her tongue, flicked the reins. Peaches walked slowly around the lot with her spindly legged foal by their side.

"This is fun." Cheyenne relaxed against her.

"It is. I started riding with my mom when I was even younger than you are. I always feel like I'm flying. Especially when I let the horse run."

"Can we run? I wanna fly."

"There's not enough room in the lot, Cream might not be able to keep up, and you need to get used to riding before we try that. It gets pretty bouncy up here when a horse runs."

They neared where Colson stood, his posture stiff.

"Can we go around again?"

"If it's okay with your dad."

"I'm having fun, Daddy. Can I go again?"

"Just one more. Cream might get tired."

As they rounded the lot again, Cheyenne chattered to the mare. "You're such a nice horse and your little baby is so pretty."

They reached Colson again and Resa reined Peaches to a stop.

"That wasn't scary at all." Cheyenne reached for Colson.

He lifted her down. "I'm so proud of you."

"Me, too." Resa swung down from the saddle and hugged Cheyenne. "You did great."

"Can I ride again tomorrow?"

"You can ride anytime you like." Resa tugged the little cowgirl hat down over Cheyenne's eyes. "As long as your daddy says it's okay. And I bet next time, he'd like to ride with you instead of me."

With a giggle, Cheyenne pushed her hat back in place.

"I'll go get the shell book for you. You can use it for the rest of your stay."

"Thanks, Resa."

"You're welcome." She slipped back into her office, gathered her things, then exited the side door and strode toward her house.

Inside, she spotted the shell book in her bookcase and pulled it out. She'd been eight when her mom gave it to her for Christmas. They'd spent hours going through it together, learning to identify shells, sorting the ones they had. It had been her mom who taught her to ride horses, too.

Poor Cheyenne. She didn't have a mom. And despite their shell sorting and horse riding, Resa couldn't fill that role in the child's life. In a week, Cheyenne would be gone.

Her heart ached. Would she ever have a family of her own? Maybe when her parents got back, everything would return to normal. Her gaze went to a shelf holding a small display of her favorite family photos.

A picture of Emmett riding his horse caught her attention. He'd been around six, and so much happier then. She missed his smile. His laugh.

Something about those eyes, that laugh… The way he tucked his bottom lip under his teeth sometimes reminded her of someone… Cheyenne. A female version of her brother as a child.

Her gaze moved to a picture of herself. Around seven, hair in pigtails, climbing the ladder to the log bunk bed her father had made for her… Cheyenne looked just like her. Resa shifted her gaze back to Emmett. Cheyenne's smile was a reflection of his. Her laugh, too. Her gestures. All this time, the child had reminded Resa of someone, but she'd never put it together. Now she could see it was her brother.

Her stomach twisted at the memory of Emmett's odd reaction when he'd learned Colson had been married. When he'd seen Cheyenne, learned she was Colson's daughter. His mention that he and Felicity had gone to the same college. And every time Emmett was around, Colson seemed jumpy. He'd admitted that Felicity had cheated on him.

Could Cheyenne be Emmett's daughter? Resa had bonded with her so quickly. Could she be the little girl's aunt? Did Colson suspect?

She grabbed the shell book and bolted for the door.

How could she learn the truth? If she was wrong, Colson would be hurt. If she was right and Colson didn't know, he'd be crushed. She'd have to handle things carefully. But the truth would come out. She'd make certain of it.

Chapter Thirteen

The bell rang and Colson hurried to answer. Probably one of the ranch hands. But when he swung the door open, and Resa stood on the porch, his heart took a dive for her. Again.

"Hey." She held a book toward him. "I brought the shell book for Cheyenne."

"Thanks." His fingers grazed hers, sending the usual jolt through him.

"Can I come in?"

"Um, sure. But I'm the only one about at the moment." He stepped aside. "Annette is helping Cheyenne get rid of her horsiness, and Dad hasn't made it home from the store yet."

"He's pulling too many hours. I really wish people would think ahead and get their Christmas gifts ordered sooner." Resa stuck her hands in her pockets and followed him to the great room. She scanned the space, homed in on a grouping of pictures Annette had set up on a bookshelf, and stepped closer.

The skin prickled at the back of his neck. What was she up to?

She picked up a picture of him, Cheyenne and Felicity. "Cheyenne doesn't look like you or Felicity. I mean, she's got dark hair like both of you. But her eyes." She focused on him. "Yours are green and Felicity's were brown."

Did she know? A chill went up his spine. "My mother had blue eyes."

"I guess eye color can skip a generation. Her mannerisms aren't like you, either, though. I can't really remember what Felicity was like in school."

"A lot of her mannerisms are like Felicity's." He grabbed the picture, set it down with a thunk. "But I'm trying to make sure she doesn't end up self-centered."

"Still. She reminds me of someone." Resa scrutinized him. "I really don't want to cause you any pain, but given everything you've told me about your marriage—" she closed her eyes "—have you ever wondered if Cheyenne might not be yours?"

"Let's go to your office." With his hand at the small of her back, he hustled her toward the door. "So we can talk without being overheard." Maybe he could get by with admitting he wasn't Cheyenne's father. Play dumb on who was. Hang on to a scrap of his secret. Hang on to Cheyenne.

Resa kept silent as he matched her quick stride to the barn. She was clearly on a mission to ferret out the truth. He might as well come clean. As they neared the building, she dug the key out of her pocket. Her hands shook as she jammed it in the lock, opened the door. He followed her inside.

"Is Emmett her father?"

No hemming and hawing on her part. "Yes."

Her eyes flashed and her jaw dropped. "Why didn't you tell us?" But despite her anger, the crack in her voice obviously came from hurt.

"I'm sorry. I wanted to."

"I can't believe this." She paced back and forth, her steps quick and jerky. "All this time, Emmett's been a father, I've been an aunt, my parents…" Her steps stalled. "She's their first grandchild and they don't have a clue she exists." She whirled toward him. "How could you keep us in the dark all these years?"

"Actually, only two years." His insides tilted. "Felicity came home drunk that last day and we argued. I made her go outside so Cheyenne wouldn't hear." He closed his eyes as her bitter words washed over him.

"She told me to not be concerned about Cheyenne…since she wasn't even mine. I thought she was just trying to hurt me, but she admitted to a fling with Emmett in college." Colson clenched his fists. "That's what we argued about right before she died. I had no idea until then."

"But you didn't tell us."

"Cheyenne was so traumatized. I knew Emmett wasn't father material, that she'd be better off with me. And I was terrified of losing her." A tic started up in his jaw muscle. "She's my little girl. Biology doesn't determine fatherhood. I've been the one to stay up with her all night when she's sick. To comfort her nightmares away. To kiss her boo-boos. She's mine."

"But if Emmett had known the truth, maybe he'd have married Felicity. Maybe he'd have grown up, become responsible, been there for Cheyenne. But we'll never know. Because Felicity lied. And you continued her lie." Resa jabbed a finger at him. "But it ends now."

Would he lose custody of Cheyenne? "Please don't tell Emmett." Something sank to the pit of his stomach. "Cheyenne will be the one to suffer. I'm all she's ever known. You can't take her away from me and give her to some irresponsible stranger."

"He's her father."

"Not to her."

Resa sighed, shook her head. "It's an impossible situation. No matter what happens, someone gets hurt. And I don't want that someone to be Cheyenne. I'll pray about it."

"Always the best thing to do. You'll let me know what you decide?"

"Yes."

"You won't do anything without letting me know your decision first?"

"I promise. For now, your secret's safe with me." The anger in her tone cooled, but her eyes turned glossy. "I can't believe you never gave me the chance to be her aunt."

"I'm sorry." He'd hurt her again. "Deep down, I wanted to, but I was scared."

She turned her back on him, but he didn't miss her quiet sniffle.

Regret stabbed deep in his chest. Yet Resa's pain was the least of his worries. He exited, strode to the house, with the weight of Texas pressing down on his shoulders. He couldn't lose Cheyenne.

The urge to grab their suitcases and flee took up residence in his brain. But where would they go? If he ran, Resa might press charges, and they'd be easy to track down in Kingsville. He couldn't uproot Cheyenne and move somewhere new. Without Dad and Annette. A life on the run.

No. He'd have to stay here. Wait it out. Hang on Resa's decision.

"Dear God, please don't let me lose Cheyenne." The vise grip on his chest tightened.

As she stood, Resa still had no clarity. She'd barely slept last night, and had spent her morning praying to God for wisdom, to help her do the right thing.

If she kept Colson's secret, she'd be living a lie. Her parents deserved to know they had a granddaughter. But if she revealed it, how would that affect Cheyenne and Colson?

And what about her brother? If she revealed

Cheyenne's parentage, would Emmett go for custody? Would he care? Or carry on with his bachelor glory days? If he didn't claim Cheyenne, would her parents seek legal rights?

She brushed off the knees of her slacks, slipped on her slingback pumps and checked her reflection in the full-length mirror. The circles under her eyes testified to her lack of sleep.

Her parents were reasonable people. They wouldn't want to disrupt Cheyenne's world. As long as Colson let them have time with her, they wouldn't rock the boat. And if Emmett claimed Cheyenne, Resa would just have to convince him that Colson needed to remain a large presence in her world.

At the core of everything was Cheyenne. Innocent and caught in the middle of this tug-of-war. Happily in the dark. It was tempting to leave her there. Except that Resa's parents had been robbed of their first grandchild. She'd been robbed of being an aunt.

Lying lips are abomination to the Lord: but they that deal truly are his delight. Her mother had drilled the verse from the book of Psalms into her heart when she was a child.

The truth needed to come out.

She grabbed her purse and headed to her office. Even though she wouldn't get any work done, she'd tell Colson her decision, make plans.

Halfway there, she saw him waiting for her. She

closed the distance between them and unlocked the door.

"Well?" His eyes were bloodshot, and his hatless hair was separated into rows, as if he'd spent a sleepless night raking his fingers through it.

"Come inside."

"I can't take another night of this. Have you decided?"

"I want you to come to Dallas with me. We need to tell Emmett together."

Colson sank into the nearest chair, as if his legs would no longer hold him up. "I can't lose her."

"I don't know what Emmett will do. Or my parents—not for certain. But if anyone other than you ends up with custody of Cheyenne, I'll personally make sure you remain in her life."

"I'm at the mercy of a whim." He covered his face with his hands. "Do you really think Cheyenne would thrive with Emmett?"

"Maybe you can relocate to Dallas. Or here, and I could insist Emmett move home, keep Cheyenne close to you. We'll work it out. And I'll help Cheyenne with any transitioning that comes up."

His hands dropped into his lap and he looked up at her, eyes full of torment. "I just don't know if I can do this."

She wanted to hug him. "I'll help you. And Cheyenne."

"Let's go today then. I hate to miss Wednesday

night Bible study, but I'd like to get this over with. Find out what Cheyenne's future holds."

"I can be ready in thirty minutes."

"Meet you at my truck."

"Sounds good."

He stood, looking beaten, and exited.

Colson loved Cheyenne as if she were biologically his. He'd known for two years that she wasn't. Yet he'd lived his life for her.

Would a judge disregard Colson's five years of love, care and commitment to Cheyenne? If so, could Emmett love her like that?

Why did doing the right thing feel all wrong?

With Cheyenne's future hanging in the balance, he'd made arrangements for the ranch chores and operations, then made the drive to Dallas with Resa. In silence.

The closer they got to Emmett's condo, the higher the wall between them became. All the closeness they'd shared officially disintegrated.

"This one. Right here." She pointed to their right.

He turned in, found a parking slot, leaned his head against the steering wheel. "You can't imagine how close I came to packing our bags, grabbing Cheyenne and running away this morning."

Her hand on his arm, she gave a gentle squeeze. "I promise we won't cut you out of her life. No matter what happens."

Maybe that could be true, but only if Emmett never learned about Cheyenne's trust fund.

Unconvinced, Colson felt his stomach give another lurch. He straightened. "Does he know we're coming?"

"Yes. I called and made sure he'd be here."

Knees wobbly Colson walked toward the condo like a man facing the gallows, with Resa's heels clicking along beside him.

"He's on the top floor."

Stucco and glass. A sleek condo surrounded by asphalt. Nowhere for a child to play. Cheyenne would be so unhappy here. But Colson would move in next door if he had to.

Surely Emmett wouldn't want a little girl to take care of, to put a kink in his carefree ladies' man lifestyle. But he might want her money.

Colson followed Resa to his doom.

She pressed the button next to an elevator. "We're here."

"Come on up." Emmett's voice crackled over the intercom and the doors slid open.

Colson endured a slow, silent crawl until the elevator stopped on the twenty-fourth floor. Resa reached toward the button to open the private elevator, but he grabbed her hand.

"Please don't."

Her arms came around his waist, and she pressed her cheek against his chest.

Warming him from the inside out. His arms slipped around her.

"It's all going to work out okay. I promise. I'll see to it. Whatever it takes to make sure Cheyenne stays happy and healthy."

"That's all I want."

"Me, too."

The door slid open. A grinning Emmett greeted them. "Well, looky here. Come on in."

Resa pulled back from Colson, gave her brother a quick hug.

He turned away, left them to follow.

With Colson lagging behind, Resa perched on a white tufted leather couch with chrome legs. Colson settled beside her, careful not to scuff the acrylic coffee table.

"Want a drink?" Emmett gestured to a well-stocked cabinet.

"You know I don't drink." Resa rolled her eyes.

Emmett's gaze shifted to him.

"I'm good."

"To what do I owe this visit?" He settled across from them in a matching chair, looking smug. "Come to ask for her hand, since our dad's not around?"

"Emmett, please. This is difficult enough. We have something very serious to discuss."

"Sounds dramatic. Is the company going under? I told you we need to go public with the stock."

"It has nothing to do with the company. It's about you."

"Uh-oh." He looked toward the ceiling. "What did I do now?"

"It's nothing you've done recently. It's what you plan to do about something you did in the past."

"Huh?" He frowned. "Can we not talk in riddles? Just cut to the chase."

"You have a daughter."

Emmett's jaw dropped and his gaze cut to Colson. He stood, stalked toward the window. "Felicity was pregnant in college. I know."

"You knew?" Resa's strained tone echoed disbelief.

"She told me it was my kid. I dumped her, gave her the money to get rid of it."

It was all Colson could do not to tackle him. If left up to Emmett, Cheyenne wouldn't have... He couldn't finish the thought.

"Oh, Emmett." Resa closed her eyes.

"It was a long time ago. I was a stupid kid." He propped his hands on each side of the window frame. "It's haunted me and I've often wondered what she ended up doing. But once you told me she married Colson, that they had a child, I suspected."

"So now that you know, what comes next?" Colson managed to keep his tone free of the rage writhing inside him.

"I'm in the process of making some changes in my life, becoming a better person, more responsible." Emmett turned to face them, strode back and reclaimed his chair.

"I'm really glad." Resa's eyes lit up, so hopeful.

"I'm meeting with my developer again tomorrow, for my video game business."

Oh yeah, all grown up. Colson's fists clenched.

"I'm working on some things, but that doesn't make me father material any more than I was back in college."

Resa shut her eyes.

"Colson's the only father she's ever known." Emmett's gaze shifted to him. "If you'll get the papers drawn up, I'll sign over all parental rights to you."

The pressure in his chest slowly dissipated.

But he had to come clean. If Emmett found out about the trust fund later, Colson couldn't go through this again. Maybe with his new business venture, Emmett wouldn't care about Cheyenne's money.

"There's something else you need to know." Colson drew in a deep breath, forced the words out. "She'll inherit a trust fund at twenty-five."

"Ol' Nigel always takes care of his own." Emmett drummed his fingers on his chair arm, as if ready for them to leave. "I'm glad the kid will be set up."

"Her name's Cheyenne." Resa's eyes turned glassy.

"Please don't look at me like that. I'm trying to do what's best for the—for Cheyenne."

And remain footloose and fancy-free.

But Colson's breathing didn't hurt anymore. "I'll get a lawyer on it."

"Just like that. Don't you want to see her?" Resa's voice caught.

"I figure she's better off if I just stay out of it. She doesn't need me complicating things. In fact, you should probably marry Colson and raise her together. It's obvious y'all are still crazy about each other."

Resa winced, shook her head.

"Take care of her, will ya?" Emmett's oh-so-familiar blue eyes closed. "I only seem to disappoint."

"I'll have to tell Mom and Dad." Resa stood.

"Do whatever you need to. Just don't include me in the new little family unit. Colson's her father."

Please don't change your mind. Colson stood, offered his hand.

Emmett shook it, then rounded the coffee table to hug Resa. "I'm sorry I can't be who you want me to be. Yet."

But was he a man of his word? Colson wouldn't rest well until the papers were signed.

Chapter Fourteen

Back on the road home, hot tears threatened as Resa kept her face averted and swallowed the golf ball–sized lump in her throat. How could her brother be so indifferent to Cheyenne? He'd known all along. Encouraged Felicity to end the pregnancy. Resa wouldn't tell Mom and Dad that part. Ever. She blinked the moisture away.

At least Colson was so elated over the turn of events, he hadn't realized how upset she was.

"I know that didn't go the way you wanted." He merged onto the interstate. "And I'd be lying if I said I'm not ecstatic over Emmett's decision, but I want you and your parents to be part of Cheyenne's life. I want y'all to be her family, her aunt and grandparents. We can figure out how to explain the particulars when she gets older."

"Really?" Resa sniffled.

"And I'll go back to King's Ranch soon, give them my resignation, arrange to put in my notice and move to Bandera."

"You'd do that?"

"Cheyenne blossomed at the ranch. With you. I want her to know y'all."

"That sounds wonderful." Resa swiped her finger under each eye. "You can stay on as foreman until Juan's return. That'll give you more time to find something permanent."

"I'll take you up on that offer."

"Thank you. And thank you for taking such good care of her all these years, for being willing to give up your livelihood for her."

"She's my daughter. Paternity has nothing to do with it."

"Obviously not, in my brother's world."

Colson turned onto an exit, then into a gas station, and stopped the truck in the lot. "Maybe Emmett's really trying to do what's right for Cheyenne's sake, so as not to disrupt her life."

"I think he's trying to do what's best for Emmett." She scoffed. "As usual."

"I don't know. When he mentioned wondering what Felicity did about the baby, I think it really haunted him. It was there in his eyes. I don't think he's as cold as he thinks he is."

"I'm glad Cheyenne has you."

"I'm glad she has us."

The softness in her eyes got to him.

Undid him. He pulled her into his arms, tucked her into his shoulder. "If I'd known I wouldn't lose her two years ago, I'd have told you then. I wish I had. You and your parents could have been making up for lost time with her. I'm sorry."

"I'm just glad you're willing to let us be part of her life now, despite Emmett's disappearing act."

"I'm sorry he hurt you."

"How will I tell Mom and Dad? This will crush them. Especially Mom."

"You'll find the words. I'll be there with you if you want. Maybe the news of a granddaughter will soften the blow."

"I hope so." She pulled away from him, mopped her face. "I'm getting you all wet."

"I can't say I mind."

Her gaze met his. With their lips so close, he could no longer resist. He closed the gap between them. Her lashes fluttered down.

Just as sweet as he remembered despite the salt of her tears. Time stood still as if he'd never left her. Never lost her. Never married Felicity and never kept a Cheyenne-sized secret from her. Six years melted away.

But then she stiffened, jerked back from him.

"What's wrong?"

"You're playing my emotions."

"Huh?"

"Making sure I'm on your side, ensuring that I don't get my parents to seek custody or court-ordered visits."

"That kiss had nothing to do with Cheyenne."

"It won't work." Resa jabbed a finger at him.

"All of my brother's schemes over the years made me an expert at detecting manipulation, so just keep your distance."

"I can't really do that as long as I'm at the ranch."

"You know what I mean. Physically keep your distance."

"Done." Nothing could happen between them, anyway—he didn't deserve to be happy. She'd just been upset. And too close.

"I think we should wait until my parents return from the cruise to tell them about Cheyenne. But I'd like to go ahead and tell Cheyenne about us and have the chance to be her aunt. That way maybe it won't be overwhelming for her and maybe we can build some excitement for her about meeting her grandparents."

He did mental backflips to keep up with her. "Sounds like a plan."

"Can I come over tomorrow after work and tell her?"

"Just don't make it a real big deal. You don't have to mention that I've known all along and kept it a secret from you. And her."

"I won't make you look bad. That would be cruel."

"Maybe you could have supper with us and tell her afterward."

"Or maybe y'all could come to my house. Mac and Annette, too. I make a mean lasagna."

"Okay." So after a family gathering over a meal, Cheyenne would learn those ties were expanding.

And then he'd be able to avoid Resa. At least until her parents returned. He just needed to refocus on Cheyenne and his job for the remainder of their stay. He'd slipped with Resa. But he couldn't let it happen again.

Coffee did nothing to soothe Colson's nerves. Maybe it would at least wake him up. He'd barely slept last night, with the kiss playing over and over in his mind. Along with her reaction to it. How could she think he could stoop so low? To romance her in order to solidify Cheyenne's custody?

Yet he couldn't blame her. She had no reason to trust any man besides her dad. Not only had Colson left her all those years ago, with no explanation, but she'd also been burned by her own brother. Coming to church with her, then hitting her up with taking the company stock public, trying to push his idea through while their parents were absent.

And Colson would do almost anything to keep Cheyenne. But not play Resa. Or hurt her. Couldn't she see how he felt about her? How he *shouldn't* let himself feel about her.

Dad shuffled into the kitchen.

"Back flaring up?"

"Yep." He poured himself a cup of coffee. "One

of these days, I'm gonna have to find another crafter to take my place. Know anybody?"

"I could do it, if I don't find a foreman job by the time Juan comes back. Either way I think I'm gonna stay in Bandera."

"Really?" Dad's eyebrows rose. "You're a natural with furniture. But would you be happy at the factory?"

"As long as I get to spend time with horses, too."

"When I talked you into coming here, you were reluctant. Even after you agreed, once you got here, you couldn't wait to leave. Now you want to stay. Anything to do with Resa?"

"It's Cheyenne. Sit down, Dad, I need to tell you something."

They settled at the ash kitchen table.

"I told you how Felicity and I argued right before she died, but I never told you about what."

"You don't have to tell me, son. It's in the past and you need to stop torturing yourself with this."

"I'm not Cheyenne's father."

Dad set his coffee cup down hard. Dark liquid sloshed over the rim.

"Emmett McCall is."

"Oh dear." Dad's hand shook as he sopped up his spill with a napkin. "Does he know that?"

Colson shared his trip with Resa yesterday. "For two years I've kept this secret, worried he'd take her away from me. That's why I fought you tooth and nail on coming here. I was afraid Resa would take one look at Cheyenne and know." He closed his eyes. "The truth finally caught up with me, but when I told him, he was completely indifferent. I should have known he was too selfish to want to raise a child. Even his own."

"That's a very good thing." Dad gulped his coffee. "He knows about the trust fund?"

"That didn't even seem to faze him. He offered to sign all custodial rights over to me. Resa recommended a lawyer here in Bandera. I'm going to see him today."

"We need to jump on this quick. Before Emmett has time to think about it and change his mind."

"I really don't think he will."

"She should have been yours."

"She is." Colson pressed a hand to his heart. "Where it counts."

"So you're staying here, so Cheyenne can be close to the McCalls?"

"They'll want to be part of her life."

"Have you told Cheyenne?"

"We're all invited to Resa's tonight for supper. She plans to tell Cheyenne she's her aunt and that Maryann and Duncan are her grandparents. But she promised to leave the Emmett part out." Dread knotted the muscles in his shoulders. "We'll figure out a way to explain that when Cheyenne is older."

"So Resa loves Cheyenne. You love Cheyenne.

And you love Resa. Why aren't you working things out with her?"

He couldn't bring himself to deny it. "It's complicated."

"You need to let go of your guilt about Felicity. She was drunk. It wasn't the horse. Felicity was in no shape to be riding even the most gentle horse in the world. And besides that, God is in control of life and death." Dad's intense gaze, the determined set of his jaw, wouldn't allow Colson to look away. "Not Colson Kincaid."

"There's more to it."

"Then what?"

"Resa believes I'll do anything to keep Cheyenne. If I even think about trying to win her heart, she'll think it's a ploy."

"Well, my son, you better figure out a way to get her to trust you then. Y'all have been pining for each other for six years. I think that's long enough." Dad pushed his chair back, turned and shuffled toward his room. "In the meantime, I gotta get ready for work."

His dad was right. Felicity had been in no shape to ride. Colson had never really thought about that before. And God was in charge. As those truths slowly sank in some of the weight lifted from his shoulders.

But Resa hated him. What could he possibly do to gain her trust?

* * *

Hands folded on his cherry desk, William Abbott had "distinguished character" down pat. Silver hair, reading glasses perched on the end of his bulbous nose, he listened intently as Colson shared Cheyenne's story.

"You're certain you're not the father?"

"Positive." Colson's jaw muscle worked overtime. "Felicity told me Emmett McCall is her father."

"But you said she was drunk and angry when she made this confession."

"Yes."

"We'll have to do a paternity test." William typed something in his computer. "I can't possibly draw up custody papers without establishing that first."

"I see. How long will that take?"

"Normally three to five days. But with Christmas, that could prolong things."

"I need this settled." Colson fisted his hands. "I can't take it hanging over my head."

"I'll try to put a rush on it."

"So what do I do? Take Cheyenne to the doctor? Do they draw blood?" His stomach turned.

"I'll set it up for you. All they do is swab inside her cheek."

"I don't want her to know what this is about. Not yet. I mean—I don't want to lie to her, but she's only five."

"I understand. We can pretend it's a flu test if you like."

"I would." Why couldn't he get the urgency of the situation across to the lawyer? "Can you go ahead and draw up the custody document, so that once we have DNA proof, Emmett can sign over his parental rights?"

"I can, but I'm afraid it's a lengthy process. Once paternity is proven, having Emmett sign custody documents is only the first step. A hearing will follow. And in the end, you'll need to adopt Cheyenne before she'll be legally yours."

Colson's lungs deflated. "So there's no way to do this quickly?"

"I'm afraid not."

"Say the paternity test proves Emmett's the father, he signs the papers, we have a hearing and I adopt her. I've seen wailing kids ripped from adoptive parents on the news. Can Emmett change his mind?"

"Technically, the process is permanent, but the biological parental rights always trump everything. It would depend on the judge."

"I see." Colson's stomach did another twist.

William picked up his phone. "I'll contact Emmett about the test and get things rolling."

But did it really matter? If Emmett was the father and didn't change his mind during the lengthy proceedings, he could still have second thoughts later. In the end, Colson would never have a legal leg to stand on. Not for certain.

Maybe moving to Bandera permanently, near both branches of Cheyenne's biological family, would nip any custody battles in the bud. Cheyenne had blossomed here. They'd be closer to San Antonio, to Dad and Annette.

It would be an easy transition. Except instead of just four more weeks to go of being around Resa, he'd be stuck in Bandera for good. If he couldn't win her trust, would his heart survive being near her on a permanent basis?

"Mmm. I love 'sagna." Cheyenne's top lip bore a tomato sauce mustache.

"Me, too." Resa's heart melted even more.

Mac winked at her. He must be upset to learn he wasn't related to Cheyenne, yet he'd come for dinner. Always supportive, always kind.

"Did Daddy tell you our news?" Cheyenne didn't wait for an answer. "We're moving to Bandera?"

"He sure did. And it makes me so happy."

She'd thought he might at least pull her aside and share how his consultation with William had gone today. But he'd remained tight-lipped, solemn, on edge during the meal.

If only they'd never kissed. Her heart did a somersault just thinking about it. She couldn't fall for him again. His only goal was to hold on to Cheyenne. Like her brother, he'd do whatever it took to get what he wanted. Any romance he pursued with her at this point would be a means to an end. To keep custody of Cheyenne. He'd probably go so far as to try to convince her to marry him if he had to.

Even with him and Cheyenne staying in Bandera, Resa had to resist his charms.

"We're still going to Singing in the Saddle Saturday, right?" Cheyenne tore her garlic toast into small bites.

"We sure are." Resa pulled off a smile, hopefully convincing.

"Ruby was talking about it at church last night. Her grandparents are bringing her and riding in our wagon." Cheyenne set her fork down. "You'll be there, right, Daddy?"

"With spurs on."

"So when are we leaving for Kingsville?"

"Not until Sunday after church."

"Just to get the rest of our stuff. Don't worry we'll be back." Cheyenne eyed her plate. "Thanks for the 'sagna, Resa. It's so good, I want to eat the rest, but my tummy isn't big enough."

"I'll put some in a container for you to take home."

"Yummy."

"Let's leave the dishes and go to the living room."

"I'm not sure I can walk away from an unclean kitchen." Annette smiled. "Why don't y'all go ahead, while Mac and I clean up."

"I hate for y'all to do that. And you're welcome to join us."

"I think the three of you need some time." Mac pushed his chair back, pulled out his wife's. There it was, sadness in his eyes. While she'd gained a niece and her parents a granddaughter, he'd lost one.

"Come on, princess." Colson helped Cheyenne down from the booster seat he'd brought. His mouth was taut, as if he wanted to get this over with.

Resa waited until Colson and Cheyenne exited the kitchen, and lowered her voice. "I'm sorry, Mac. I know this must be hard on you."

"It's not your fault."

"None of this will change anything. Cheyenne loves you, and in her heart, you're still her grandfather."

"Are you sure Emmett will sign the papers?"

Her heart clenched. "I'm certain he has no interest in raising her."

"And that hurts you."

"I'm fine." A lump formed in her throat and she swallowed hard. "As long as I can be her aunt." She kissed his cheek. "She'll get another set of grandparents, but it won't change anything for you."

"Thank you for letting us stay in her life." Mac gave her a quick hug.

"Whatever's best for Cheyenne." She smiled, patted his cheek. "The disposable containers are in the island. Be sure she gets plenty of leftovers to take home." Resa turned away and headed for the living room, past ready to break the news to her niece.

Colson and Cheyenne sat on the couch with a cartoon turned down low.

"Hope you don't mind I switched the TV on." Dread shone in Colson's eyes.

"It's fine." She sank to the empty seat beside Cheyenne.

The little girl turned from the TV, glanced around the room. "I just love all your horse stuff."

Resa picked up a turquoise suede throw pillow with a horse silhouette and fringe, then gestured to the matching window treatment. "All of this came from the store. We have lots of bedspreads with horses on them. You could have one." She hugged the pillow. "But right now, I have something exciting to tell you."

Cheyenne turned from the television, looked up at her, so trusting. "What?"

"I'm your aunt."

"Really?" Cheyenne smiled, her eyes wide. "Did you go on 'cestry dot com and find out?"

Resa frowned. "I'm not sure what that is."

"Ancestry dot com. Cheyenne's babysitter in Kingsville was researching her family tree," Colson explained.

"Oh." Resa laughed. "Something like that."

"So can I call you Aunt Resa?"

Her vision blurred. "I'd love that."

Cheyenne hugged her. "This'll be fun. I've never

had an aunt before. Well, except my mommy's sister, but I don't ever see her."

"You can plan on seeing me a lot. And guess what? My parents are your grandparents."

"Wow." Cheyenne pulled away. "But Grandpa Mac and Nette are my grandparents. And Gramps, too. And Mimi." Hyacinth—the afterthought.

"Yes. Plus two more."

"What about the man sitting with you at church once? Grandpa Mac said he was your brother."

Resa's breathing stilled. Had Cheyenne sorted out her family ties? "He doesn't come home very often."

"Is he my—"

"We'll sort it all out later." Colson cut her off.

"But he's my uncle, right?"

That was a close one. Her gaze met Colson's over the top of Cheyenne's head. His face had paled, his lips tautened.

"Something like that." Resa's sigh slipped out. "But like I said, he doesn't come home much. You probably won't meet him for a while."

"When do I get to meet my new grandparents?"

"They're still on the cruise. But they'll be home next week. On Christmas Eve."

"I can't wait."

"Me, neither. They'll be ecstatic to meet you."

"Thank you, Daddy." Cheyenne beamed at him.

"For what?"

"This is why we're moving here. So I can be with

my new aunt, grandparents and uncle." Cheyenne's brow puckered. "Wait. Since you're my aunt, does this mean you can't be my new mommy?"

Resa's jaw dropped. Her brain stalled.

"Someday I might get married again, princess." Colson cleared his throat. "But Resa will always be your aunt. And always be a part of your life."

"Okay, but if you wanted to, could you marry Resa, Daddy? Even though she's my aunt?"

"If she wanted to, I could."

"Good." Cheyenne clapped her hands.

"But—"

Annette and Mac stepped into the living room, cutting off Resa's protest.

"I've got leftovers." Mac held up a bowl. "And the kitchen's all clean. How's everything in here?"

"Guess what, Grandpa?" Cheyenne bounced off the couch, ran into his legs. "Resa's my aunt and I got more grandparents."

"That's wonderful, munchkin. More people to love you."

"But you and Nette are still my grandparents, too."

Mac's chin trembled. "And you're my favorite granddaughter."

"Oh, Grandpa. You're just saying that 'cause Nette's grandkid is a boy."

"Let's go." Colson stood, grabbed Cheyenne's coat from the entry closet. "Resa probably has some work to do."

"I'm finished for the day."

"We need to go, though." He helped Cheyenne into her coat. "This little girl needs to get into her jammies. Bedtime soon."

"Bye, Aunt Resa." Cheyenne waved. "See you tomorrow."

Resa's eyes grew moist again. "See you then, sweet pea." She blinked the tears away, focused on Mac. "Thanks for cleaning my kitchen."

"No worries." He shot her a wink, then ushered Annette out.

When the door shut behind them, Resa grabbed a tissue and let the tears roll. The emotional evening had taken its toll. On top of yesterday's disappointment in Emmett. And in Colson. But Cheyenne had taken the news in stride. Kids were so resilient. If only adults could be.

Chapter Fifteen

As the evening sun slipped below the horizon, Colson wrapped up his day. But it didn't matter now. Even after he finished his stint at the ranch, he'd be in Bandera. Too close to Resa, since she'd probably never trust him.

His heart was still lodged in his boots from Cheyenne asking about her relationship to Emmett. His little girl was too smart for her own good. Added to that was her Resa-as-her-mommy dream. His insides were ripped to shreds. So much for eating, sleeping, thinking.

He just needed to get through Singing in the Saddle tomorrow and the trip to Kingsville. He'd be back in Bandera the day before Christmas Eve. Only a day before Maryann and Duncan's homecoming. Before Dad and Annette would go back to San Antonio.

Colson had booked a suite for him and Cheyenne at the dude ranch next door until he could find a permanent place in Bandera. He'd have to find a job, too. Once Juan returned in mid-January, he could probably fill in at the local store as a crafter.

He strolled to the house. Tugged his boots off in the mudroom.

So many changes. A month ago, he'd never have thought Cheyenne could adapt. But she was all excited about meeting her new grandparents and moving to Bandera.

In the great room, Dad swung a golf club in a smooth stroke. "Always gets the kinks out."

"Where's Cheyenne?"

"In the kitchen with Annette."

"I'll get a hug, then go pack. By the time we get back, y'all will be getting ready to return to San Antonio."

"Maybe not." Dad set the golf club in the corner. "Annette and I are talking about moving to Bandera, too."

"What about her teaching job?"

"She's a small-town girl and word is there's a sub position opening up in Bandera next year. One of Annette's former principals is there now, which makes her a shoo-in."

"Y'all would uproot your lives for us?" Colson felt his chest squeeze. His father had always been so supportive. Done his best to make up for Mom leaving.

"You should know by now, it's what parents do. I never wanted to move to San Antonio, always planned to retire here."

"Why did you move, then?"

"For you. I knew you'd gotten in with the wrong crowd." Dad grimaced. "I thought moving would give you a fresh start."

"Wow. I never knew that." Colson sank into a chair.

"I've always loved it here, and I figure I've missed out on too much of Cheyenne's life as it is."

"What about the San Antonio store?"

"We have a great manager there and I've been grooming Lonnie and a backup crew for years." With a hand to his lower back, Dad eased into a chair. "He's done a stellar job in my absence and I'm ready to cut down on my workload. I'm thinking two or three days a week is enough. Duncan's thinking the same thing. In fact, before the renewal ceremony, he approached me about tag-teaming it at the Bandera location."

"Maybe once Juan returns and I deliver my notice in Kingsville, I could give you both a break until I find a foreman position."

"My back will take you up on that."

The doorbell rang.

"I'll get it." Cheyenne came barreling out of the kitchen. "Daddy!" She veered toward him, forgetting all about the door.

His heart pooled as he scooped her up. Resa might be her favorite aunt, and she'd soon meet her new grandparents, but he was still number one in Cheyenne's book. For now.

Mac went to open the door, and Colson could hear Resa's voice in the foyer.

"Aunt Resa!" Cheyenne scrambled out of his arms.

"Hey, sweet pea." Resa knelt and wrapped her up in a big hug. "I have an idea."

"What?"

"Instead of you going to Kingsville with your daddy Sunday, maybe you could stay with me."

"Yay!" Cheyenne bounced up and down.

As Colson's chest caved in. "I'm not sure that's a good idea."

"Let's go see how supper's coming." Mac held his hand toward the little girl.

"I wanna stay here with Resa, Daddy."

"We'll talk about it." His jaw twitched.

"Come on, munchkin," Mac pressed. "I bet it's time to do the garlic toast and I always burn it."

"I'll help you." Cheyenne clasped his hand.

As they strolled to the kitchen, Colson caught Resa's elbow, hustled her toward the door.

"Hey." She jerked away from him.

"Outside. Now," he barked.

She stepped out, turned on him as he shut the door behind them. "You don't order me around."

"You may be Cheyenne's aunt, but you still run things past me." He jabbed his thumb against his chest. "Are we clear?"

Her gaze dropped to his shirt collar. "I'm sorry.

I should have asked you first. I got excited and it slipped out. I have to stop doing that."

He hadn't expected her to go all contrite. His anger ebbed in the face of her apology.

"You're right, I should ask you first on anything concerning Cheyenne." Resa bit her lip. "So can she? Stay with me, I mean?"

And he wanted to kiss her. For loving Cheyenne. For being impulsive. For being Resa.

He took a step back. "My leave doesn't end until February, so it doesn't make much sense to drag Cheyenne with me just to make arrangements for my notice, then turn around and come back here. If she wants to stay with you, she can."

"Thank you." Resa gave a little bounce, much like his daughter's, then closed the gap he'd made and hugged him.

He held her fast. Close to his heart. Right where he'd always wanted her.

The door opened. "Supper's…" Dad fell silent.

Resa pulled away from Colson, patted his shoulder. "He's letting Cheyenne stay with me. If she wants."

"I'm glad." His dad's perceptive gaze jumped from her to Colson. "Wanna stay for some leftover lasagna? You can give Cheyenne the news."

"I've got plenty of lasagna at my place, but I would like to tell her." Resa practically bolted inside.

"Looks like you took my advice," Dad whispered.

"What advice?"

"Working things out with her. Getting her to trust you."

"She was just excited because I said yes, so she hugged me."

"Uh-huh." His dad reentered the house.

Colson followed.

Could he win her trust? Could he finally gain the affections of the woman he'd loved for six years?

The tangible tug-of-war inside Cheyenne made Colson regret coming as he sat on the tailgate of his truck with her in his lap.

How could he help make her feel safe and secure enough to ride in the wagon pulled by horses? He'd thought her riding Peaches would make this a nonevent. Until she'd gotten a glimpse of the huge draft horses attached to the wagon lined with multicolored Christmas lights.

Butch and Dutch patiently waited, their gray coats shining and their black tails swishing.

"It's up to you, princess."

"Can't a truck pull the wagon, Daddy? Like when we went to Lights on the River."

"I'm afraid not. We can watch the carolers leave from here if you want. Or we can go home."

"But I want to go caroling, Daddy. Can we follow in a truck with the windows down?"

"They only allow horses, buggies and wagons."

"Hey, Cheyenne." Resa strode toward them. "Aren't the horses awesome? Did you know they're specifically made for pulling wagons and buggies? It's in their bloodline. Most horses instinctually try to run from anything you hook them to unless you spend lots of time training them." She hopped up on the tailgate, settled beside them. "But these horses are born for it. Nothing scares them."

"Are they your horses? I haven't seen them at the ranch."

"They belong to a neighbor, but he always lets us use them for the parade and caroling."

"Do you know what kind of horses they are?" Colson asked.

Cheyenne surveyed the huge draft animals. "Blue roan Percherons."

"Wow. Very impressive horse knowledge." Resa high-fived her. "Lots of people mistake them for Clydesdale grays."

"But Clydesdales have white feet, not black."

"You talk like your daddy's a horse whisperer."

Used to be, anyway. Colson held in a scoff.

"But they're just as big as Clydesdales." Cheyenne's gaze didn't budge from the team.

"They have to be big to pull a wagon that'll hold eighteen to twenty people. They're gentle giants." Resa focused on something in the distance and her face lit up. "Ron, Becca, I'm so glad you came. And so glad you brought Ruby."

"Ruby!" Cheyenne almost dived off the tailgate, but Colson caught her.

"Careful." He slid down, set her on the sidewalk.

A middle-aged couple strolled toward them, each holding one of Ruby's hands.

"Ruby can't wait to ride in the wagon. Thanks so much for inviting us," the woman said.

"This is Ron and Becca Fletcher, Ruby's grandparents," Resa explained. "They work at Chase and Landry's dude ranch next door. This is Colson Kincaid, our temporary ranch foreman, and his daughter, Cheyenne."

"We've heard so much about Cheyenne." Becca smiled.

"I told Grandma about your French braid." Ruby inspected Cheyenne's hair.

"My daddy did it for me, but Resa showed him how. Maybe she can show your daddy."

"But my mommy does my hair."

"Oh." Cheyenne closed up a bit.

"I'd be happy to show your mom." Resa hopped down from the tailgate. "It's time to get in the wagon. Caroling begins in just a minute."

"Are you coming?" Ruby held her hand toward Cheyenne. "I've never ridden in a wagon before."

"What about the horses?" Cheyenne mumbled.

"I love horses. I ride all the time at the dude

ranch and Daddy's thinking about buying me one. I want a buckskin. Do you know what that is?"

"Tan-colored hide, black mane and tail. Palominos are my favorite. I rode one named Peaches with Resa once, then rode her several times with my dad." Cheyenne squeezed his hand. "Come on, Daddy, let's get in the wagon."

Colson's jaw dropped as she clasped Ruby's hand with her free one.

"There's my little pumpkin." Nigel knelt in their path to the wagon.

The little girl stiffened as she neared her grandfather, and clenched Colson's hand tighter. "Are Mimi and Jasmine coming?"

"I'm afraid not. They don't really do wagons."

Her grip relaxed. "Can I sit in your lap, Resa, with Ruby and Grandpa beside me?"

"I think that can be arranged."

Which booted Colson right out of the picture.

He ended up across from Resa and Cheyenne. With a straight-on view of them both. Of the bond getting stronger between them.

As Cheyenne grew even more attached, his heart longed for Resa.

The only thing certain in all this craziness was that Resa wanted nothing to do with him. He needed to get through this hayride. And hightail it to Kingsville tomorrow afternoon. Maybe twenty-four hours away from her would clear his head. And help him figure out a way to win her heart. So his would stay intact.

"Colson." Marshall shook his hand. "You look good."

"I feel good." He sat in the chair across from his boss's desk. "You were right. I needed a leave."

"Ready to come back?"

"About that… Being near my daughter's family in Bandera made me realize she needs them."

"Honestly, I was afraid you'd end up relocating over this."

"I'll complete my current job in mid-January. After that, I'm willing to give you whatever notice you need. A month, several months. This place has been good to me. I don't want to leave you in the lurch."

"Don't get me wrong. We miss you around here—especially as a horse whisperer. But Walker is a great foreman. In fact, he asked me the other day if you were coming back and said if you didn't, he'd like the job on a permanent basis."

"That was easy." Colson adjusted his hat as a dream ended. All his years of longing to be a horse whisperer at the largest ranch in Texas… But the realization of that dream hadn't fulfilled him. All he needed to make him happy was Cheyenne. And Resa. But if he couldn't win her heart, her trust, how could he be content being near her?

"Unless you want to hang around just for fun, there's no need for you to fulfill any kind of notice. We're good here. And I'll give you an excellent reference."

"Then I'll pack the rest of our things, head out in the morning," he answered.

"Suit yourself." Marshall stood, offered his hand. "We'll miss you around here."

"I appreciate everything." But Colson wouldn't miss anything. Everything he wanted and needed was in Bandera.

If only he could convince Resa of that.

As he exited the office, he punched in her number so he could talk to Cheyenne.

"Hi, Daddy. Are you coming home yet?"

"Not till tomorrow, princess. I have to pack all the stuff we left in Kingsville and get it loaded in the trailer."

"I miss you, Daddy."

"And I miss you, princess." So much his breathing had been off since he left her. "Are you being good?"

"Really good. And I'm going to work with Resa tomorrow. When will you be home?"

"Sometime after noon."

"Bring my Barbie house."

"I will. I'll call you again later. I love you." So much.

"I love you, too, Daddy."

He ended the call, climbed in his truck. Maybe

the rush on the DNA test would come through and the custody papers would be ready before Christmas. His best gift ever. If Emmett signed them.

No if about it. Emmett had to sign them.

After that, Colson wouldn't have to worry about Cheyenne calling anyone else Daddy. Unless Emmett changed his mind. But he couldn't let himself think that way and still function.

On the way to their cabin, he passed where they'd lived with Felicity. Where she'd died. He'd passed the place daily for two years and it always took the wind out of him. This time, he stopped, parked in the drive. Walker lived there now, but he was busy being the foreman, so no one was home.

Colson got out of his truck, strode to the back of the house, to the fence. With their argument hot and heavy in his memory, he leaned on the top rail, buried his face in his arms. Felicity's scream, watching the horse rear up, her crash into the mud. His boots sinking in the muck as he ran to her. Her neck at an odd angle; Cheyenne's little face pressed against the window...

"I'm sorry, God. For the mistakes I made with Felicity. For not loving her. For arguing with her. For any part I had in her death. Maybe the horse was safe, but I should have kept her from getting in the saddle. I never meant to hurt her. We were miserable, but I didn't want her to die. Forgive me. Help me to forgive myself."

A burden lifted as he continued to pray. "Help

me to do the right thing by Cheyenne. To be the best father I can be to her. Erase any memory she has of that horrible day. Forgive me for hiding the truth from the McCalls."

He raised his head. Far out in the pasture, a horse and rider cantered toward him. As they neared, he recognized the buckskin gelding by his gleaming cinnamon-colored coat, black mane and tail, muscled legs. The horse Felicity had ridden that last time.

The rider was a young girl, maybe ten years old. Walker's daughter, Marla.

"Mr. Kincaid, you're back?" she called.

"Just packing our things. We're moving to Bandera permanently."

"Oh." Her expressive face left little to his imagination. She knew her dad had his job, and she was thrilled about it. Then manners kicked in. "Sorry to see you go."

"Thanks. You ride Winston often?"

"Almost every day. He's a great horse." She patted the buckskin's shoulder. "Somebody was hunting nearby the other day when I was riding him. Several shots were close, but Winston never even flinched. Dad says all your horses are the best trained. You gonna go back to horse whispering in Bandera?"

"Maybe." And for the first time since Felicity's death, he could consider it.

The horse stamped a foot, obviously restless.

"See you later." Marla turned away, let Winston run. Smooth gate, calm and serene carriage… All he needed was a sober rider.

Colson wouldn't miss this place, but he did miss his work with horses. Could he find a job horse whispering in Bandera?

But even more than he missed working with horses, he missed Cheyenne. And Resa.

Chapter Sixteen

"I can't believe we could play all the rest of the afternoon and you wanted to come back to my office after lunch." Resa flipped the light switch, ushered Cheyenne inside and shut the door. "On Monday. Most people don't like to work on Monday. And besides that, it's almost Christmas Eve."

"Let's design something." The child went over to Resa's drafting table.

"I'm fresh out of orders at the moment. All the Christmas designs are finished products and I'm ahead into the New Year on my work. The week of Christmas I always have a break."

"Let's design something, anyway. Just for fun."

"Well, I have been trying to think of something new to put in the store. Got any ideas?"

"A toy box."

"That's great!" Resa hung their coats on the rack, then pulled up Rustick's inventory on her computer. "We have several, but we could come up with a new one."

Pictures of several log and barnwood chests popped up on her screen.

"How about something with a lid, like a treasure chest."

"Sure. We have to make the lid really lightweight with a special hinge so nobody gets hurt. But we could round it like a treasure chest. Anything else?"

"Put kids' names on it." Cheyenne rolled her eyes. "I can't ever find anything with my name on it."

"Another great idea. You're really good at this. I can never find anything with my name on it, either." And it had always frustrated her.

"And you've got deer pictures and horseshoes, but what about a cat or a dog or a ballerina."

"You're right, not all kids like deer or horses. Maybe some sports symbols, too—like a baseball bat, a basketball." Resa made notes.

"Or badminton or tennis."

"I foresee a job at Rusticks for you in the future. As a designer and in the ideas department."

"I wanna be a designer just like you, Aunt Resa."

"I think we've got a lot of good ideas here, Cheyenne. But what do you say instead of working, we go up to the loft and meet my cat and her kittens?"

"There's kittens up there?" Cheyenne gave her characteristic bounce.

"Half a Stache, Pinocchio and their mom, Moonpie."

"Those are weird names!" Cheyenne giggled.

"You'll understand once you see them. Come on."

She tugged her coat on, helped Cheyenne with

hers, and hand in hand, they stepped out of the office, into the wide galley between the stalls and over to the ladder.

"Can you climb up okay?"

"I love to climb."

Resa waited until Cheyenne was halfway up, then followed to make sure she got up into the loft safely. "Careful. Hold on to the railing."

The sweet scent of hay and fresh crisp air greeted them as they stepped up onto the planked flooring.

"Sit here." They settled on a hay bale side by side. "Kitty, kitty, kitty, kitty," Resa called in a singsong voice.

A kitten popped over a hay bale. "That's Pinocchio. He has a black nose, so it looks like it's really big." Resa picked up the furry little animal and handed him to Cheyenne.

"It does!" she exclaimed.

Another kitten and the mama cat darted from the rafters.

"Half a Stache has a black smudge on his nose that looks like half of a mustache. And Moonpie is their mama."

"They're so cute. How long have you had them?"

"Moonpie is three and the kittens are six weeks old. They've just gotten to where you can cuddle them good."

"I love them."

"Have you ever had any pets?"

"There were cats and dogs at the other ranch. But they weren't mine."

"Well, these cats like living in the barn. But if your daddy says it's okay, maybe one of the kittens can be yours."

"Maybe both of them."

"And you can visit them whenever you want. As long as you get an adult to come with you."

"I'm so glad we're staying here instead of going back to Kingsville." Cheyenne snuggled Half a Stache close.

"Me, too, sweet pea." Resa didn't know what she'd do without this child. If only Cheyenne wasn't a package deal. She could definitely do without Colson in her life.

"Hello?" a familiar male voice called from below. Emmett!

"What are you doing here?" Resa's insides went cold.

"Mom and Dad are coming home tomorrow. Remember I said I'd be here, go to the airport with you?"

"Is that Uncle Emmett?" Cheyenne scampered to the loft window.

"Um, just go on to the house. I'll be there in a minute." She had to keep Cheyenne out of his sight. If he actually saw her up close and personal, would he change his mind about relinquishing his parental rights?

Was it really fair to ask him to sign over custody when he'd gotten only a glimpse of her? But it should be Colson's call on when and if Emmett got near Cheyenne.

"I want to meet him," Cheyenne whined.

"There's plenty of time for that. I'll just run you over to Annette, since I need to discuss some things with my brother."

But she knew it was too late when she heard scuffling on the ladder and Emmett's head popped up through the hole in the loft floor.

"Hi, Uncle Emmett." Cheyenne waved.

Emmett went still, his gaze fastened on her. Then he lost his grip and bobbed around.

Resa gasped. "Careful."

Regaining his hold, he steadied himself. "Hey, kid."

"I said go on to the house and I'd meet you there."

"I'm already up." His eyes never left Cheyenne. "I'm Emmett."

"I'm Cheyenne. I never had an uncle before."

His sad gaze met Resa's. "I've never been an uncle before."

"Come see the kittens."

Emmett climbed the rest of the ladder and stepped into the loft.

Cheyenne gave him a hug. "I'm glad to meet you."

"Me, too." He awkwardly patted her on the head.

He was playing it cool, like he always did. But

Resa knew deep down he was on edge. The pain in his eyes and tautness of his jaw proved it.

"The kittens are named Pinocchio and Half a Stache." Cheyenne grabbed his hand, tugged him toward the hay bale where they'd been sitting. "Have you seen them before?"

"No." Emmett settled on a bale. "I'm not really a cat person."

"Here." Cheyenne gently picked up the kitten and held it toward him. "Half a Stache likes to cuddle."

Emmett reluctantly took the little black-and-white ball of fur from her. It was more than Resa had ever managed to get him to do.

"My daddy used to not be a cat person, but then he held one."

Was that regret that flashed in his eyes? Did he regret not being Cheyenne's dad? He couldn't change his mind about giving her up. This could be bad.

"This one's Pinocchio." Cheyenne leaned her head against Emmett's shoulder.

That flash of something in his eyes again… He cleared his throat. "So do you have some papers for me to sign?"

"Not yet." She could've cried with relief. Started breathing again. "So are you staying for Christmas?"

"Probably."

"You should stay. I can't wait to meet my new grandparents."

"So what do you want for Christmas, kid?"

"A pony."

"Really?" Resa's eyes watered up.

Emmett caught her reaction. "What's the big deal about that?"

"Cheyenne used to be afraid of horses."

"Until I rode one on a carousel with Daddy and Aunt Resa. And then Aunt Resa took me to pet Cream. That's Peaches's baby. And then we rode Peaches together." Her little face grew animated as she spoke. "And then I rode with Daddy. It was so much fun. I wanna do it again."

Emmett's gaze shifted back and forth between them, as if he craved the bond they shared.

"Cheyenne? Resa?" It was Colson's voice, coming from below.

Her breathing skittered to a complete halt.

"Daddy. Up here. In the loft."

The cat and kittens scattered.

"Cheyenne, hurry down, so your daddy doesn't have to climb up." *So he won't see your real daddy here.*

"But I want Daddy to see the kittens."

"They won't come out with all the hollering. He'll have to see them another time."

Resa shot Emmett a desperate, silent plea—*Stay up here.*

He splayed his hands, kept sitting there, as if her world wasn't on the verge of going off-kilter.

She escorted Cheyenne to the ladder, started

down, then helped her to follow, ready to catch her if she fell.

"Daddy." Cheyenne ran to him as soon as she reached the ground.

He picked her up, swung her around and around as she giggled.

"Now I'm dizzy." When he set her down, she wobbled.

He knelt, held her steady with a hug. "I missed you, princess."

"I missed you, Daddy."

"If you'd stayed gone any longer, I think I'd have had to bring her to you." Resa smiled, trying to act natural.

"Thanks for keeping her." His jaw set, he looked up at the loft ladder.

"Anytime." Suspicious. Had he heard Emmett's voice?

"Did you bring my Barbie house, Daddy?"

"I did. It's in your room. Waiting."

"Thanks for keeping me, Aunt Resa. I had big fun." She gave Resa a quick hug, then tugged Colson toward the house.

"Bye, sweet pea." Resa kept a smile pasted on her face until they rounded the barn, out of sight.

Emmett climbed down the ladder. "I'm guessing you didn't want him to know I'm here."

She covered her face with her hands. "I'm toast."

"Why?"

"If he finds out you're here, he'll think I set up this meeting between you and Cheyenne."

"Didn't you? Trying to force fatherhood on me? It won't work. I'm signing the papers."

She frowned up at him. "I had no idea you were coming."

"We planned this before Mom and Dad left."

Oh yeah. She'd forgotten all about that plan. "That was a lifetime ago."

"You're telling me her being here for my arrival was an accident? No hidden agenda?"

"Hidden agendas aren't my MO."

"Touché." His Adam's apple knotted up. "You really forgot?"

"My brain's pretty much been out to lunch since I learned the truth about her."

"I don't want to complicate things."

"You won't. Just don't do an about-face on the custody papers."

"I won't." Emmett stared off into the distance. "But she's a pretty cool kid. As far as kids go."

"He's done a great job with her. You need to let him continue."

"I will." Her brother turned away.

"You're not leaving, are you?"

"Isn't that what you want?"

"No." Yet part of her wanted him to. For Colson's peace of mind. For Cheyenne's sake. But Emmett couldn't just stay away permanently. Not without hurting their parents. "I want you to be here for Mom and Dad's return tomorrow. Like we planned."

"But what about Colson?"

"I just need to smooth things over, ease into it gently that you're here, that it has nothing to do with Cheyenne."

"If he gives you any trouble, you let me know."

"He won't."

"I'll be at your house. Or should I get a room?"

"My house is fine."

He disappeared around the side of the barn.

Judging by his reaction to meeting Cheyenne, Colson didn't have a thing to worry about. Yes, Emmett had been tense, and she'd seen flashes of regret in his eyes, but he was much too focused on himself to raise a child. And if it came to it, she'd testify to that in court.

Cheyenne belonged with Colson. A man who'd given up his life dream to raise a little girl, who wasn't even his.

The *Bonanza* theme started up and she dug her phone from her pocket. William Abbott. "Hello?"

"Resa, I have papers for Emmett to sign and I can't get in touch with him. He listed you as a contact."

"Emmett is here at the ranch. He probably forgot to charge his cell."

"If he can come by my office, he can sign them today."

"Thank you, William. He'll be there. Have you called Colson yet?"

"I'll contact him once Emmett signs the document. Once both have signed the original, I'll file the order and take it from there. Merry Christmas."

"Merry Christmas." She slid her phone back in her pocket. The perfect Christmas gift for Colson.

If they were going to share Cheyenne, they needed to at least get along.

Was there a new man in Resa's life? Colson strolled back to the house with Cheyenne's hand safely in his. He'd definitely heard a man's voice in the loft. And she hadn't wanted him to come up.

"So what were you and Resa doing in the loft, princess?"

"Seeing the kittens."

"What else did y'all do while I was gone?"

"Yesterday we colored, sorted shells again and went to church last night. Today I helped her design a new toy box. And then the kittens. And then Uncle Emmett came and I got to meet him."

Emmett? Colson's blood boiled. "What was he doing here?"

"I guess he just came to visit. He came up in the loft, but the kittens ran when I hollered at you from up there."

And Resa hurried Cheyenne down and tried to hide him.

They reached the house. "I need to go back and check on something I forgot to ask Resa. You go on inside and I'll be back soon."

"Okay, Daddy." She hugged him tight. "I'm so glad you're home."

"Me, too." He kissed her soft cheek, drew in her scent, then set her down and watched until she scampered safely inside.

As he stalked back to the barn, a red Ferrari roared out of Resa's garage. The personalized plate caught his attention: 4U2 NV. For you to envy. Very fitting for Emmett.

Without knocking, Colson jerked her office door open, rattling it with his force, and skewered her with a glare.

She was sitting at her desk. Her mouth opened, then closed. "What?"

"Busted."

"I totally forgot he was coming." She closed her eyes, shook her head.

"More like you weren't expecting me back so soon." He closed the gap between them in two jerky strides, leaned toward her. "You have the nerve to accuse me of playing you, then as soon as I turn my back you arrange for Emmett to see Cheyenne, hoping he'll change his mind and want her."

"That's not what happened."

"Why then? Why is he here?" His gut twisted. "Did it work? Is he challenging me for custody now?"

"He's here because Mom and Dad get back tomorrow. We planned it before they ever left. I just forgot."

"You forgot?"

"My parents are coming home. Tomorrow is Christmas Eve. We're having a big family gathering the next day. They're about to learn Cheyenne is their granddaughter, that they missed out on five years of her life, because Emmett wasn't man enough to step up and be her father. Then or now."

Colson's hands shook. "He doesn't want her, now that he's seen her?"

"William Abbott called a few minutes ago. The papers are ready and Emmett just went to sign them. And this will all be over with."

Why hadn't the lawyer called Colson? That must mean the test proved that Emmett was the biological father.

"Why can't you believe that I'm on your side on this?" Resa asked him. "I truly believe Cheyenne is better off with you."

She was good at bluffing. But he wasn't falling for it. Even if Resa hadn't invited Emmett here, she'd hoped he'd fall in love with Cheyenne and raise her. But it hadn't worked. Her brother was colder than she realized. Thankfully.

Colson's silence had her fidgeting.

"All I want is for Mom and Dad to be happy and for Cheyenne to be part of our lives."

"Despite your recklessness with my daughter, it looks like you got your wish."

"She's my niece. I'd never do anything to hurt her."

"She's my daughter!" he roared.

She jumped.

"In every way that matters," Colson went on. "And I'll do everything in my power to protect her. You can be part of her life, but Emmett gets near her only when I say so. Are we clear?"

"Abundantly." A tear slid down her cheek.

He was immune. Or pretended to be, anyway. "We'll be all cleared out by the time your folks arrive."

"Will you bring her for Christmas?"

"I'll think about it." He stalked to the door and stormed out. But he was all bluff, too. He'd take Cheyenne to her new grandparents for Christmas. He'd cave whenever Resa wanted to spend time with her.

Because even though she couldn't fully be on his side against her brother, her tears bored a hole straight through his heart. Especially when he caused them.

Chapter Seventeen

Emmett pulled his Ferrari into the circle drive with a roar and stopped at the front door of Mom and Dad's house. Resa let go of the breath she'd been holding and managed to extract herself from the back seat, while Dad helped Mom out.

While they'd gone to the airport, Mac and Annette along with Colson and Cheyenne had checked into Landry and Chase's dude ranch next door.

"You really should get a more sensible car, son." Dad shook his head.

"Guess I should have let Resa drive hers to pick y'all up." Emmett didn't kill the engine after he popped the trunk.

"You're staying, aren't you?" Resa ducked to get a glimpse of him.

"I have a few errands to run. I'll be back."

"We should have stopped at the grocery store." Mom started for the house, then paused. "Will you pick up a few things?"

"Annette left the fridge stocked and cooked soup for us before they left. I put it in a pot on the stove, ready to warm up," Resa assured her.

"Oh, good." Mom clasped a hand to her chest. "That's so sweet."

Dad shut the passenger door, went around to dig out the luggage. Hands full, he headed to the house. Mom took a rolling case from him.

"Let me help." Resa grabbed the carry-on.

"Hey, Resa." Emmett revved the engine.

She stepped back to the Ferrari, ducked to see him through the open window. "What?"

"Can you tell them? About Cheyenne."

Her insides quaked. "Shouldn't you do that?"

"You said you would."

"But that's when I forgot you planned to be here."

"I can't face the disappointment in their eyes. And you have such a way of…smoothing things."

She closed her eyes. "I guess. But you're coming back, right?"

"I'll be back tonight. I promise." His tinted window slid up and he roared out of the drive.

Inside, it felt like home again, with Mom already warming the soup. Dad stashed the suitcases in the foyer and sat at the breakfast bar, while Resa made coffee.

"I brought these for you." She slid the financial reports from the store and the ranch over to him.

"You know me well." He opened the file for the store first.

Keeping her eyes on Mom, Resa dived in. "Did y'all ever think of going public with the company stock?"

Mom laughed. "Emmett actually came up with that a few months ago, talked your father into bringing it up." She rolled her eyes. "Along with setting up our corporate offices in some ridiculous San Antonio high-rise."

"Your mother set me straight in no uncertain terms." Dad grinned. "Helped me remember that we're a local, small-town, family company. Fortune five hundred doesn't fit us."

"I'm so glad y'all are back." Resa was all teary. From relief, and the bomb she had to drop. "Sorry to hit you with business so quickly."

"I had the time of my life on our cruise, but there's no place like home." Mom clicked her heels together with a grin. "And business is part of that."

"Are you tired?"

"Maybe a little jet-lagged." Dad set the report aside. "Looks like somebody did an excellent job during our absence. I knew you could handle it. Be honest, how much was Emmett here while we were gone?" Dad's tone was grave. He obviously wasn't expecting much.

"He was here every time we were shorthanded." Okay, so that was only once, but still the truth.

"I knew he could do it." Mom's smile was priceless.

And now Resa had to single-handedly rip it off her face. She set a mug of coffee beside each of her parents, then carried hers over and claimed the seat by Dad.

"About Emmett. I have to tell you something."

"If it's bad news, can it wait until after Christmas?" Dad sighed.

"It really can't. But it's actually good. Sort of." Good that they got Cheyenne out of the deal. Bad that they'd missed out on having her all these years.

"Just tell us." Mom sipped her coffee. "I don't want anything hanging over us for two days."

"I invited Colson and Cheyenne over after lunch. They'll be here in a few hours."

Her parents looked at each other, then her.

"Colson is here?" Dad frowned. "Did we miss something while we were gone?"

"It's not what you think. There's nothing going on between Colson and me." She quickly explained about Juan's leave and Colson filling in during his absence.

"You should have called us." Mom added another spoonful of sugar to her coffee. "You were supposed to call us if anything went wrong. Why didn't Juan say anything before we left?"

"Juan and Mac worked it out, and he didn't say anything because he knew y'all would freak out and cancel the cruise."

"We would have," Dad admitted. "But it would have been the right thing to do. You shouldn't have been here dealing with all of this alone."

"I'm fine. The ranch is fine. The store is fine."

"It must have been a shock when Colson showed

up with Cheyenne." Mom rounded the island, settled on the other side of Resa at the breakfast bar.

"To be honest, I almost swallowed my tongue."

"I guess we should have told you." Mom patted her knee. "But you were so heartbroken."

"Y'all honored my desire to never hear his name again."

Dad sighed again. "We weren't sure how to handle things. Never could decide if you were better off kept in the dark or knowing the truth."

"I'm not sure myself." Clueless about Cheyenne, she'd been angry and hurt, which had effectively killed the love she'd felt for Colson. If she'd known why he'd married Felicity back then, she might have still loved him, and ended up pining for a man she couldn't have. It was a toss-up. "You did what you thought was best. I'm okay with that. None the worse for wear."

In the end, Felicity had ripped their love out from under them with a lie. But if Colson hadn't married her, what would have become of Cheyenne?

Resa sipped her coffee, willed it to settle her nerves. "Have y'all ever met Cheyenne?"

"No." Mom shrugged. "Every time we got together with Mac about the business, either here or in San Antonio, Colson was never around."

"She's a living doll."

"We'll look forward to meeting her."

Resa drew in a calming breath. "She has coloring similar to mine—dark hair, blue eyes. In fact, several people mistook her for my daughter over the last three weeks."

"Felicity had dark hair and so does Colson. I don't remember either of them having blue eyes, but Colson's mother did. Not piercing like yours, but blue nonetheless." Mom fiddled with her coffee cup. "I wish Mac and Annette could join us for lunch. I should have called them."

"They're coming for the big meal tomorrow." Resa reached for her parents' hands. "This is important."

"You're making me nervous." Mom clasped her fingers. "Please, just tell us what's going on."

"Felicity cheated on Colson."

"That's terrible." Mom frowned.

Resa's gaze bounced back and forth between them as she waited for them to put it together. Nothing. "With Emmett."

Mom's hand went to her heart. "You mean—?"

"Cheyenne is Emmett's daughter?" Daddy's jaw dropped. "Our granddaughter?"

"Yes. Colson's bringing her over for lunch, so y'all can meet her."

"Does Emmett know?" Mom's chin trembled.

"This is the hard part. Apparently Felicity told him when she learned she was pregnant." Resa squeezed Mom's fingers. "And he dumped her."

"Oh my." Her mother's tears came.

Resa let go of their hands and passed her a tissue. "Felicity passed the child off as Colson's and he married her. He didn't know the truth until shortly before her death."

"But that was—" Daddy clenched his teeth "—two years ago. He's known all this time and didn't tell us?"

"He had no idea Emmett knew about the baby all along. He was afraid Emmett would take Cheyenne away from him if he learned he was her biological father. For three years, Colson thought she was his. By the time he learned the truth, she *was* his—in his heart. He hated hurting us, hiding the truth, but he couldn't bear the thought of losing her."

A muscle in Daddy's jaw flexed. "So what now?"

"Emmett still has no desire to be a part of her life." She filled them in on the trip to Dallas with Colson, the custody agreement, Cheyenne's visit with Emmett. "Emmett signed the papers yesterday. Cheyenne knows I'm her aunt, that y'all are her grandparents, but she thinks Emmett is her uncle. Colson wants it to stay that way until she's older. Until he can figure out a way to explain that her biological father never wanted her."

"I should've jerked a knot in that boy's tail years ago." Daddy closed his eyes. "I guess he's not staying for Christmas."

"He promised me he would. He'll be back tonight. Hopefully, we'll have a nice Christmas gathering tomorrow. Colson is bringing Cheyenne, and Annette and Mac are coming, too."

"And we're all supposed to tiptoe around the

fact that our son is an irresponsible, deadbeat dad."
Resa's father spewed out a heavy sigh.

"Maybe we can hash that out tonight, when Emmett gets back." Mom tried to remain positive, but her faith in her son was obviously waning.

"It's not complete selfishness. I mean, yes, he's not interested in putting himself aside to raise a child, but he also knows Cheyenne is better off with Colson," Resa stated. "He knew back when Felicity initially gave him the news that he wasn't father material, and felt Cheyenne would be better off without him."

"So he wants what's best for her. And for himself."

"I'm sorry." She patted Daddy's hand. "I know you're disappointed in him. I am, too. But you have a granddaughter and she's the sweetest thing."

"Resa is right." Mom dabbed at her eyes. "Our first grandchild."

"And we've missed out on knowing her for five years." Daddy's hand fisted.

"Let's focus on the positive, Duncan." Mom mopped her face, then hopped off her stool. "I need to go freshen up before they arrive. Oh my, we don't even have any Christmas gifts for her."

"I bought some things."

"Oh, good. Will you take care of the soup while I get myself together?"

"Sure." Resa stood, rounded the island, lifted the lid to stir. "Mmm, tamale soup."

Daddy stayed at the breakfast bar, his shoulders slumped.

"Please don't be angry or sad. Let's just forget the years we lost, forget our disappointment and focus on Cheyenne and what a blessing she'll be in our lives."

"I'm trying, sweetheart." Her father stood. "Maybe I need to go jog on the treadmill, blow off some steam." He patted her hand as he headed for the stairs. "I'll get it together before Cheyenne arrives, I promise."

He might. But at the moment, Resa wanted to rage at her brother. He should have been the one here in the hot seat, confessing his sins. But he'd begged her to clear the air for him before his arrival tonight. And she'd done it. Just like she'd always tried to smooth things over for him.

"Please ease tempers, disappointment and hurts, Lord. Help us to have a peaceful family Christmas. Put our focus on Cheyenne, on You and counting the blessings You've given us."

Peace eased the tension in her shoulders.

In a few hours her parents would meet their five-year-old granddaughter for the first time.

Her cell chimed and she checked the display: William Abbott. "Hello?"

"Resa, I'm sorry to bother you again, but I'm having the same issue I had yesterday. I've been trying to get in touch with Colson Kincaid, but I'm not getting an answer on his cell. I know he's living at your folks' home, so I'm wondering if you've seen him."

"He's moved to the Chasing Eden Dude Ranch since my parents got back today. If you can't reach him there, he's coming here after lunch, so I can tell him to call you."

"Yes. Please do that."

She knew just how to break the news.

Dread boiled in Colson's chest as he pushed the doorbell. Only yesterday he'd strode into this house whenever he wanted, slept here, ate here. But Duncan and Maryann were home now, waiting to meet Cheyenne.

"Do you think they're home, Daddy?" Cheyenne fidgeted.

"They should be."

The door swung open and there stood Resa. Her loveliness took his breath away. If only her brother didn't stand between them.

"Hey, Cheyenne." She knelt to her level. "Ready to meet my folks?"

"Uh-huh." Cheyenne nodded, hands clasped in front of her, twisting her upper body from side to side.

"They're in the great room."

"That's my favorite room." Cheyenne tugged on his hand. "Let's go meet my new grandparents, Daddy."

It was incredible how much she'd blossomed in

just three weeks, from a shy young girl who ran from strangers. He loved her new openness, but in truth he just wanted to scoop her up and run himself.

In the great room, Duncan and Maryann sat side by side on the sofa.

Maryann gasped. "Oh my goodness, she looks just like Resa at that age."

"'Cause she's my aunt." Cheyenne clung to Colson's leg.

"I promise we don't bite." Duncan chuckled. "Especially not our first grandchild."

"I'm Cheyenne." She let go of his leg, inched toward them. "It's awful nice to meet you."

Maryann patted her lap. "I've wanted a little granddaughter for years. Wanna sit on my lap?"

"Or maybe just here between us till you get to know us better." Tension eased from Duncan's features and a genuine smile took over.

Cheyenne grabbed Resa's hand. "Can I sit on *your* lap?"

"Of course." Resa led her to the couch.

Duncan and Maryann scooted apart, made room for them. Resa settled between her parents, and helped Cheyenne onto her lap as the child sized up the hovering adults.

"I really like your dress." Maryann adjusted the lace hem. "Pink is my favorite color."

"Mine, too. How come you're crying?" She eyeballed her grandmother.

"Well, like I said—" Maryann leaned forward, grabbed a tissue from the box on the coffee table "—I've wanted a granddaughter for a long time. So I'm happy."

"Oh, they're happy tears."

"Definitely."

"You remind us so much of when Resa was little." Duncan patted Cheyenne's knee. "Now she's all grown up, so we're thrilled to have a little copy of her."

"I have lots of grandparents." Cheyenne looked around at her captive audience. "Grandpa and Nette are awesome. And I like Gramps Nigel. But Mimi makes me nervous."

Colson tried not to cringe. He'd have to break the news to them soon.

"I've known Hyacinth my entire life." Maryann dabbed at her eyes. "It's just her way. But I'm certain she loves you. How could anyone not love you?"

"Can I still sit in your lap?" Cheyenne peered up at her.

"Of course, sweetheart. I've waited my whole life to hold my first grandchild. And I'll try not to get you wet."

"It's okay." Cheyenne crawled into Maryann's lap. "Daddy says happy tears are the best kind."

Resa stood and gave Duncan room to get closer. Cheyenne didn't even notice, so taken with these new enamored adults.

"Your French braid sure is pretty." Maryann smoothed a few wayward strands back in place.

"Resa showed Daddy how to do it."

And just like that, he was back in that moment. With Resa braiding Cheyenne's hair that first time. His fumbling hands grazing hers.

She still got to him. But if he couldn't trust her with Cheyenne, he sure couldn't trust her with his heart.

Resa strolled over to the Christmas tree, then knelt and started digging out presents. "Since everyone will be here tomorrow, we thought now would be a good time for Cheyenne to open her gifts from us."

"Y'all got me something?"

"Of course we did." She stood, arms full of brightly wrapped boxes, set them on the coffee table, then swiped at the knees of her slacks.

Would they spoil her just as badly as Hyacinth had Felicity and Lucinda? Colson wondered. He'd have a talk with them before things got out of hand.

"We got y'all something, too." Cheyenne grinned at all the presents. "But not this much."

"Since we've been gone, Resa did our shopping for us, and she might have gone a little overboard." Duncan handed her a box. "But we're just so happy to have a granddaughter. This one's from Resa."

"Open it first." Resa knelt on the floor next to her mom.

Cheyenne tore into the paper. "A shell book like

yours. I love it. Now I don't have to borrow yours. Thank you."

"But we can still study the book together and sort shells when we get some new ones."

"We need to get some new ones soon." Cheyenne clasped the book to her heart.

"Open these next." Maryann handed her a package wrapped like a huge piece of hard candy with the paper twisted at each end and a ribbon holding it in place. Then pointed to another just like it.

Clinking sounds emerged as Cheyenne unwrapped the paper to reveal a huge bag of shells. "I love shells."

"Resa told me. We picked these up for her during our cruise, but decided ya'll can share them. One bag is from Greece and one from Portugal. I put notes inside, so we'd know which was which when we sort them."

Ten minutes later, a pile of wrapping paper and ribbon littered the floor. Three dresses, a coat, a pair of shoes and a new Barbie... Considering the fact that the McCalls had missed out on Cheyenne's first four Christmases, Resa really hadn't gone crazy with it.

"Here's yours, Colson." Duncan held a box wrapped in faded blue toward him. Not Christmas paper.

"Me? You didn't even know I was here and you certainly didn't have to get me anything."

"He picked this up for you a long time ago and

the way I see it, we owe you the world for taking care of our granddaughter all these years." Maryann leaned her head against Cheyenne's.

Colson's heart warmed as he accepted the gift. The McCall's weren't holding it against him that he'd kept Cheynne from them.

"Open it, Daddy."

He tore the paper away to reveal a book. *"The Faraway Horses."* Reverence took his breath. "By Buck Brannaman."

"Who's that, Daddy?"

"He's a really great horse trainer. So great, he inspired a movie. And inspired me."

"Is that *The Horse Whisperer* guy?" Resa picked up wrapping paper, stuffed it in a large trash bag.

"I went to one of his clinics after high school. It changed my life." He ran his hand over the cover. "Thank you."

"I bought that book the spring you worked here and had a friend who attended one of his clinics get Buck to autograph it for you. Was gonna give it to you, but never got around to it," Duncan murmured.

Because he'd left.

"And you kept it all these years." Even though he'd broken Resa's heart. Colson opened the book, ran his fingertips over the signature.

"I couldn't bring myself to throw away an autographed book, so it ended up in the attic. Forgotten. Until today."

Colson closed the book, met Duncan's gaze. "I'll treasure it."

"This one says it's from Resa, Daddy."

"You got me something, too?" His chest went all soft inside despite the tension between them.

"It was last-minute."

Cheyenne handed him a brightly wrapped shirt box.

He ripped the nativity scene paper away, removed the lid, to find an official-looking document inside. Had Emmett changed his mind? Was it an order to turn Cheyenne over to him? Colson's heart stopped and his hands shook as he scanned the legal jargon. But it wasn't that. He saw Emmett's signature at the bottom—signing his parental rights over to him.

"What is it, Daddy?"

"Nothing, princess." *Everything.* He clasped the document to his chest. "Just some papers."

Cheyenne frowned at him. "That's a weird gift."

Laughter clogged in his throat. "It's exactly what I wanted. Thank you, Resa." He sought her gaze. If she was all for Emmett raising Cheyenne, why would she give him the papers?

"It's just a copy." She gave a stiff shrug, looked away. "Did William Abbott get in touch with you?"

"My cell phone belonged to King's Ranch, so I had to turn it in. Cheyenne and I went for a horseback ride this morning, got back in time to change clothes and come here."

"He said to call him. He'll probably be willing to meet you tonight, even though it's Christmas Eve."

She'd given him the thing he wanted most, even after engineering the meeting between Emmett and Cheyenne. Though Colson was starting to rethink that. This wasn't the kind of thing a woman with an agenda would do. "I have something for y'all, too." He picked up the three gift bags he'd brought in with him. "Can you pass them out, princess?"

Cheyenne bounded over to him, grabbed the bags, handed one to Resa and one to Maryann.

Both women dug through tissue paper Cheyenne had carefully placed in the bags.

"Oh my." Resa clasped a hand to her mouth.

Maryann had much the same reaction.

"They're memory books, with lots and lots of pictures of me to fill the pages with."

"I thought Cheyenne could help y'all put the pictures in."

"I don't know what to say." Maryann's voice caught.

"I figure since y'all missed a lot of years, this might help." He gestured to a third bag by his feet. "I got one for Hyacinth, too, with copies of all the pictures for her."

"That's so thoughtful." Resa's eyes were damp. "Thank you. I'm sure Hyacinth will love it."

"Can I invite Gramps Nigel to Christmas here?" Cheyenne piped up. "And I guess... Mimi, too?"

Colson's nerves went into overdrive. "Mind your

manners, princess. We don't invite extra guests to someone else's house." And Emmett's presence would be enough to deal with. The Birminghams could not come. Not unless he told them the truth first.

"Actually, that's a very nice idea." Maryann shifted Cheyenne's weight. "I'll call and invite them."

Resa's eyes widened, caught his gaze. "I'm not sure we'll have enough food, Mom."

"Oh, of course we will. The café always has those huge trays." Maryann gave Cheyenne a squeeze. "Next year, I'll let you help me bake a turkey. But this year, since we just got home, we're having our Christmas dinner catered by the dude ranch next door."

But Colson couldn't even think about food. He couldn't risk the Birminghams hearing about Cheyenne's connection to the McCalls at the Christmas gathering. And he couldn't ask everyone involved to lie.

There was no choice. He'd have to come clean. Tonight.

"Can we talk?" Resa whispered.

Duncan and Maryann were so focused on Cheyenne, they didn't know anyone else existed.

"Sure." Even though it wasn't on his wish list.

"Outside." She ushered him into the hall, grabbed their jackets.

They stepped out without the others noticing.

"Before you start yelling." She settled on the porch swing. "I didn't think to tell them Hyacinth and Nigel don't know about Emmett."

"I'm done with yelling. And with secrets." Colson chose a chair to her right.

"I think we've had enough of both." Her words came out clipped.

He looked up into the sky, layered with puffy white clouds. "Did Emmett tell you he had to have a paternity test before he could sign her over to me?"

"No. But I guess it makes sense."

"The lawyer asked if it was possible for me to be her father. I'd never considered that after Felicity's confession. But for a moment, I allowed myself to dream. It was a good dream." He closed his eyes.

"It doesn't matter now. She's yours," Resa said.

"She is. And I'm grateful. But I'm still so scared of losing her. What if Hyacinth decides to cause trouble."

The porch swing creaked. "Want me to go with you to tell them?"

Could he trust her motives? "I'll handle it."

"Look, I'm not excited about spending time with you, either, but since we're both part of Cheyenne's life, we need to get used to it. And I don't want Hyacinth getting any ideas about custody."

What agenda could she have, other than trying to help? Hyacinth and Nigel might have even more legal right to Cheyenne than Duncan and Maryann, since they were her maternal grandparents. Maybe he did need backup.

"Okay."

Resa's jaw dropped. "I'll go tell them we're running an errand. Cheyenne will be fine here." She stopped the swing. Stood.

"What time will Emmett get back?"

"Not until at least seven or eight."

"You're certain?" He studied her face, searching for the tiniest hint of duplicity.

"I promise."

"I'll go in with you, let her know I'll be gone for a little while." But she wouldn't miss him.

As more people crowded into Cheyenne's life, Colson couldn't help feeling as if he was losing her. He'd been the center of her universe until now. Even if no one challenged him for custody, the people in her world were multiplying faster than his wary heart could keep up with.

Adding to his unease was Resa. He'd bawled her out yesterday and today, she was still helping him. Despite his misgivings, his heart was shifting back in her favor.

Chapter Eighteen

"I can't believe you kept this from us." Hyacinth dabbed her eyes with a handkerchief.

This wasn't going well. Nerves tingling, caught up in someone else's drama, Resa was at a loss on how to help.

"First you kill our daughter. And then you fail to tell us you have no biological ties to our granddaughter."

"Stop it, Hyacinth." Nigel's tone held warning. "You saw the report on Felicity's blood alcohol level. She had no business getting on a horse."

"But he didn't stop her." Hyacinth jabbed a finger at Colson.

"Did you ever try to stop Felicity from doing whatever she set her mind on? Not an easy task, especially when she was drunk. And I suspect Colson was trying to take care of Cheyenne that day. Felicity certainly never paid her any mind."

"She didn't get drunk very often. He drove her to it."

"Stop pretending. You know our daughter was out of control."

Hyacinth's fuchsia-tinted lips opened, closed, as if she realized her argument was only revealing family secrets.

"Felicity is gone." Nigel's eyes were glossy. "The point is, we know the truth now. It's how we handle things from this moment forward that matters."

"We'll file for custody. As soon as Christmas is over." Hyacinth's jaw set with determination.

Resa's heart dipped. "Surely you don't want to disrupt Cheyenne's life like that. Colson's been the only constant in her world. He's moving here so that all of us can be near her. And Emmett signed custody over to Colson. Can't we just leave Cheyenne's living arrangements as they are?"

"We certainly can." Nigel folded shaky hands in his lap. "And we will."

"We most certainly won't," Hyacinth snapped. "She's our granddaughter. And he stole her from us."

"No more histrionics, Hyacinth. You don't want to raise Cheyenne. You only want to add her to your collection of pretty possessions, to be raised by a nanny. The child will stay with Colson. Period."

"How dare you speak to me this way?" His wife clasped a hand to her heart.

"It should have been done years ago. If you so much as glance at a lawyer regarding Cheyenne's custody, I'll cut off your monthly stipend."

Hyacinth's mouth clamped shut. She stood, stalked from the room.

"I'm sorry." Colson ducked his head. "I know this is hard. I should have told y'all long ago."

"You didn't because you were afraid she'd sue for custody. That I'd sit on my hands and let her. But I'm tired of letting her run over me. Cheyenne will stay with you. And that's final."

"Thank you."

"I only want what's best for my granddaughter. And this household isn't it."

"Cheyenne wants you—and Hyacinth—to come to my parents' for our Christmas meal. At one tomorrow," Resa said.

Nigel's eyes went soft. "I'd like that. If I can cool Hyacinth down by then, make sure she'll behave, we'll be there. If not, I might just show up alone."

"Sorry to disrupt your evening." Colson stood.

"I'm sorry for the things Hyacinth said to you. Her father spoiled her terribly. I'm afraid I carried on the tradition rather than face her wrath. But no more."

"Please come tomorrow." Resa slipped into her jacket. "Cheyenne really likes you."

"The feeling is mutual."

"There is one more thing." Resa chose her words carefully. "Cheyenne knows I'm her aunt, that my parents are her grandparents, but she doesn't know how we're related. She assumed Emmett is her uncle and we let her. For now."

"There's no reason to foist such complicated matters on a five-year-old. If we come, I'll make sure

Hyacinth holds her tongue." Nigel offered Colson his hand. "Thank you for taking such good care of our granddaughter."

"I love her."

The two men clasped hands.

Outside, Resa strode toward the truck. "I'm glad Nigel found his backbone. He's a nice man."

"I'm glad he's on our side." Colson cleared his throat. "Are *we* on the same side?"

She turned to face him. "I told you, I'm with you on this. Whatever's best for Cheyenne. And I'm convinced you're it."

"No hidden agendas? No getting close to her, then calling a lawyer? No trying to convince Emmett he should take responsibility for her?"

"She belongs with you." Tears pricked Resa's eyes. "I don't know why you can't believe me."

"The same reason you don't believe I kissed you in Dallas because I wanted to." He held his hands up in surrender. "With no agenda."

Her heart squeezed at the memory. "Because we've both been hurt in the past."

"Maybe it's time to stop letting past hurts color our future. I'm sorry about yesterday. I jumped to conclusions when I realized Emmett was here and overreacted."

"Yes you did." She skewered him with a look. But deep inside, she wanted to trust him. And he wanted to trust her. How could she build a relationship with a man who assumed she'd betray him and harbored issues as big as her own? "We better get back and check on Cheyenne."

"I'm supposed to meet William at his office to sign the papers, anyway."

"And you need to make sure she's out of range when Emmett arrives. I think Daddy's going to explode on him." She turned away, opened the truck door, climbed inside.

With no answers about their future. For either of them.

Raised voices came from Daddy's office. Resa cringed as she paced the great room.

"Do you think we should intervene?" Her mom was perched on the sofa and Resa saw her wince. "It sounds bad in there."

"They'll work it out." Hopefully. "They always do. It's been a very eventful Christmas Eve. At least Colson and Cheyenne escaped long before Emmett arrived."

"Yes." Mom wrung her hands. "Your father's always been so hard on that boy. And I've always been too soft."

Resa plopped down beside her. "I think he's really trying to grow up. He's starting a video game business."

"That's grown-up?"

"The business part of it is." She sighed. "I'm just as disappointed as y'all are, but we need to support him, instead of questioning everything he does. And bashing him for everything he doesn't do."

"You're right."

The door to Dad's office swung open and Emmett stepped out. "Sorry, Mom, guess I'm not staying for Christmas, after all." He bolted for the front of the house.

"Wait!" Resa shot after him.

But he could always outrun her. She didn't catch up with him until he'd already climbed into his Ferrari. She planted herself in front of it, crossed her arms over her chest.

"Come on, get out of the way!" he shouted.

Resa shook her head. "You can't leave. Tomorrow is Christmas."

"Yeah, well, I can't take another Christmas as the black sheep."

"Just talk to me."

He stared her down, but a click sounded as he unlocked the doors. "Get in."

She ducked into the passenger seat, shut the door, leaned against it. "Mom needs you to stay."

"Dad made it obvious he wants me to go."

"No, he doesn't. He's just—"

"Disappointed. I've always been a disappointment to him. Especially compared to the golden child. I could never live up to your standard. Or his."

"I'm not the golden child."

"Trust me, you are."

"You wanna know the reason I think you and Daddy have issues?"

"Enlighten me."

"You're too much alike. Both stubborn and bull-headed, intent on your own way. While Mom and I run around trying to smooth everything over."

"You may be onto something, oh golden one."

She punched him in the shoulder. "Families are supposed to be together this time of year."

"I don't know. With Cheyenne and Colson coming, this might be the perfect Christmas for me to skip."

"But you can't." She squeezed her eyes shut. "Not after I've used up all my smoothing ideas. Colson thinks I arranged for you to come meet Cheyenne, so you'd change your mind and want to raise her yourself."

"Whoa. So your love life is as trashed as mine at the moment?"

"I don't have a love life. Never have."

"You love him."

"Even if I did, he doesn't trust me. And the feeling's pretty mutual."

Her brother leaned back against the headrest. "I'm sorry I've made such a mess of things."

"I'd believe that, if you'd stay."

"You're relentless in your smoothing."

"Please. I'll help you with Daddy."

"All right. But this might be too big a job for even you."

He might be right.

"Since you're staying, I'll give you a heads-up. Nigel is probably coming tomorrow, and possibly Hyacinth, too."

"This just keeps getting better and better." Sarcasm rolled off his words. "Do they know about me?"

"Colson told them last night."

"So Nigel's bringing his shotgun?"

"He actually took it quite well. I think he was angrier at Hyacinth's reaction than at you."

"I sure wish I'd done things differently." Emmett closed his eyes in turn. "I never dreamed my recklessness would still cause reverberations over five years later."

"Lapses in judgment come with consequences." She drew in a deep breath. "But Cheyenne is a blessing. God can take our worst moments and let something good come from them."

"All the same, I know you have this dream Christmas vision." He squeezed the steering wheel until his knuckles went white. "But I'm not sure I should be part of it. Maybe I need to get out of Dodge, steer clear until things settle down."

"You can't duck out and leave us to face your reverberations. That's cowardly."

"You always know how to hit a guy where it hurts. So Hyacinth is livid?"

"Pretty much. But Nigel handled her, surprisingly well."

"You don't think they'll try to take Cheyenne away from Colson, do you?"

She scoffed. "Hyacinth raise a child?"

"Yeah, you're probably right." Her brother rested his hand on the gearshift, as if still wishing for escape. "But if it comes to that, I'd testify on behalf of Colson."

Resa's insides warmed. Maybe Emmett was growing up. Though he didn't feel up to the task of raising a child, he obviously wanted the best for Cheyenne. And was smart enough to see that Colson was the right choice.

Even after being neighbors and friends with the Donovans her entire life, Resa still felt odd just walking in the Chasing Eden Dude Ranch back door without knocking. Completely furnished with Rusticks furniture and decor, the place had proved to be a great advertisement for the store.

In the large kitchen, staff scurried, serving guests in the dining room and filling catering orders.

"Your order is ready, Resa." Landry picked up a stack of three pans. "I'll help you carry it out."

"I'll take that." Chase swooped in, tried to take her load. "Don't want you overdoing it."

"I'm fine." Landry turned away from him. "Besides, I need to tell Resa."

"Tell me what?"

"Hand it over." He scooped the load from Landry

and motioned to a stack of three more pans. "Can you get those, Resa?"

She picked them up. "Tell me what?"

"Can you get the door, Landry? The car door, too."

Landry hurried ahead, opened the back hatch of her SUV.

Chase slid his boxes inside, then took Resa's load, set them next to his pile and closed the hatch. "I'll cover for you while you tell her." He jogged back to the kitchen.

"Tell me what?"

Landry patted her stomach. "I'm pregnant."

Resa clasped a hand to her heart. "Oh, that's so wonderful." She hugged Landry. "I'm so happy for you."

"We just found out. You're the first to know besides our families. We're keeping it quiet for a few months, but I couldn't leave you in the dark."

They leaned against Resa's SUV side by side.

"When are you due?"

"The end of July. So tell me about you?"

"I held down the fort. Mama and Daddy got home safely." Resa counted five decorated cedars in the expanse of yard behind the dude ranch.

"I heard Colson's sticking around. Anything to do with you?"

"Long story. I'll fill you in soon, but he's staying here because of Cheyenne."

"I'm guessing that's what went wrong with y'all

in the past. He fell for someone else and that's why we don't like him."

"That's what I thought all these years." Resa brought her up to speed on their whirlwind romance, him leaving her without a word, marrying someone else.

"So Felicity must have been pregnant. He did the right thing. You can't fault him for that."

"No. But I'm not sure I can trust him, either."

"I'm not following. You know anything you tell me will go no further."

"Turns out Emmett is actually Cheyenne's father. Colson found out two years ago, but Emmett signed her custody over to him yesterday."

"We definitely need to get together more." Landry shook her head. "How did I get so behind? But I still don't understand why you don't trust him."

"What if he's afraid Emmett might change his mind, or Mama and Daddy might sue him for custody? What if he kissed me because he wants an edge? To use me to keep my family at bay."

"He kissed you?"

"Focus. What if?"

"Like I tell my cynical sister, love takes a leap of faith and starts with trust. If you don't take that leap, you're destined to be alone." Landry squeezed her hand. "I don't want that for you."

"I'm really happy for you and Chase." Resa patted Landry's arm.

"We're ecstatic." Her friend's smile was luminous. "But I better get back inside and help in the kitchen."

"We have to get together soon."

"We will." Landry hugged her, then headed for the ranch house.

A silver car pulled in beside Resa and Landry's sister, Devree, got out.

"Hey, how's the best wedding planner in Texas?"

"Up to here with weddings." Devree stretched a hand high over her head. "Did you hear the news?"

"Your sister just told me. I'm so happy for her and Chase."

"Me, too. I really am." Devree rolled her eyes. "I'm just not sure I can take so much happily-ever-after."

Resa grinned at her. "Well, I better get going or our meal will be cold. Merry Christmas!"

"You, too."

Resa got in her car and started for home. What had made Devree so pessimistic?

If given the chance to choose between cynical and alone or happily-ever-after, Resa would pick the latter. But was she brave enough to take that leap of faith that began with trust?

Everyone Colson had tried to hide Cheyenne from for the past two years was behind this door. The urge to grab her and run bubbled inside him. They all knew the truth now. Any or all of them had the power to rip her away from him. Rip his heart to shreds.

But he'd met with William Abbott, signed the papers last night and petitioned to legally adopt Cheyenne. Surely that meant something.

Christmas was supposed to focus on Jesus. But as Colson stood on the porch with his daughter, his dad and Annette, dread rushed through him with every beat of his heart.

"Relax, son." Dad clapped him on the back, then lowered his voice. "You've got the law on your side now."

Annette gave him an encouraging smile.

The door whooshed open and Resa greeted them. "Merry Christmas. Everybody's waiting for our favorite princess."

Cheyenne darted inside, bolted toward a waiting Maryann and Duncan.

"Everyone's here?" Colson whispered. "Emmett? Hyacinth?"

"Present and accounted for."

"Why do I feel as if I'm entering the lion's den?"

"Emmett's on our side. Last night, he told me that if Hyacinth gives you any trouble, he'll testify on your behalf."

The vise grip around Colson's heart let up.

"And Hyacinth is harmless—Nigel's threat of hitting her in the pocketbook worked wonders." Resa closed the door behind him. "Besides, God will go in any lion's den with you."

"We're almost ready." Maryann took Cheyenne's hand and turned toward the kitchen. "Just give us a few minutes to get the lids off and the utensils out."

Colson ended up helping Cheyenne fill glasses with ice. A few minutes later, steaming pans lined the counter, with a circle of guests standing around the large kitchen. He caught a glimpse of Emmett, Hyacinth and Nigel. "It's ready, people." Duncan clasped his wife's and his daughter's hands. "Let's pray."

Everyone gathered bowed their heads.

"Thank You, Lord, for this food, and for the birth of Your son, who came to die for our sins. Thank You for this family, our guests. Thank You for another year of Your boundless blessings, and most of all for Cheyenne. Amen."

Minutes later, plates filled, they lined the long dining room table. Cheyenne sat between Colson and Resa, with Emmett on his sister's other side. Maryann, Hyacinth, Mac and Annette were across from them, with Duncan and Nigel manning each end. For once in her life, Hyacinth seemed to have taken a vow of silence. A nice reprieve.

"Did you get what you wanted for Christmas, kid?" Emmett leaned around Resa to see Cheyenne.

"Daddy said I needed to practice riding some more before I get a pony. But I got lots of other cool stuff."

As she went through her list, with detailed descriptions, Colson's tension eased. Emmett talked to her like she was just some random child. Completely casual, as if she was nothing special to him. Yet that he spoke to her at all meant that wasn't the case.

Colson could live with that.

As he relaxed, his taste buds kicked in and he actually enjoyed the meal—plus the pleasant conversation around the table, Cheyenne being the center of attention, watching her bloom. Maybe having more people to love her wasn't such a bad thing.

Especially Resa.

"I've got cleanup." Resa stacked plates as everyone pushed away from the table.

"No, you don't." Maryann gathered silverware. "I didn't even have to cook. You young people go relax."

"Yeah, um, I've got a thing." Emmett headed for the door. "I'll be back later."

And Colson relaxed even more.

"I'll help." Annette went after the glasses. "Maryann can tell Hyacinth and me all about the cruise."

"Thank you for the catered meal." Hyacinth's uppity nose twitched dismissively, as if it was beneath her palate. "But we really must be going. I feel a headache coming on."

"I'm not ready to leave yet." Her husband focused on Cheyenne.

"You can go, Hyacinth. I can bring Nigel home," Colson offered.

The woman harrumphed. "Fine." She flounced from the room. "I can see myself out."

"What do you say Mac, Nigel and I take princess duty? Piggyback time." Duncan stooped with his back toward Cheyenne as she filled the room with giggles.

"I'll help the ladies." Colson picked up a stack of plates.

"I'll let you carry them into the kitchen, but then you shoo." Annette waved him away, cast a furtive glance at Resa.

Her gaze met his. With all their parents looking on.

"Go for a walk or something. You both worked so hard while we were gone." Maryann chuckled. "But watch out for the mistletoe. Your father stuck it everywhere yesterday."

Resa's face turned scarlet. She scurried for the mudroom.

Colson would have to hurry to keep up. But finally, after all this time, his heart was up to the challenge. He just needed her to forgive him.

The footfalls behind Resa were accompanied by Colson's familiar spicy scent. She really hadn't expected him to follow.

"I thought I'd go up to the loft." She slipped her coat on, while he dug his out. "Check on my cat and her kittens."

"Cheyenne's really excited about them." He

opened the door for her, followed her out. "I expected this to be the worst day of my life. I honestly pictured everyone grabbing one of her limbs and pulling her apart like a wishbone."

"We're all a pretty civilized bunch." Resa zipped her coat. "Feel better now?"

"Much. Emmett's and Hyacinth's disinterest make me feel like maybe this whole thing can work out." Colson grimaced. "Great. I just insulted your brother."

"You weren't insulting him, just stating the facts." Maybe she'd be able to breathe better with him out of her space. "You don't have to come with me. Go play with Cheyenne or watch sports on TV."

"I'm good. Cheyenne will want a kitten report." He matched her stride.

Resa took in a deep breath, tried to get her lungs working in a natural rhythm. Why did being near him make her want to forget all their differences? "Any news on the job search?"

"I plan to apply at several ranches in the area for a foreman position. But I've been thinking I might apply as a horse whisperer, too."

She stifled a gasp. "I'm glad. You're so good with horses." Was he healing? Forgiving himself?

"In the meantime, I'm giving our dads some relief as a crafter at the store. I might need a refresher course. It's been a while. I'm definitely rusty."

"Like riding a bike. You'll be back up to par

in no time. I know Daddy wants to cut down his hours, and your dad's back has been acting up."

They reached the barn, and Colson waited while she filled a container with water. When she climbed up the ladder, he followed.

The mama cat darted toward her, kittens in pursuit.

Resa knelt and scratched her cheek, then refilled their food and water dishes. Tasks finished, she strolled to the back loft window and plopped down with her legs hanging over the ledge. The mama cat rubbed against her elbow until Resa picked her up, snuggled her against her chest. "Emmett used to dare me to jump from here."

"Did you?" Colson sat beside her.

"I had to. It was a dare." She grinned.

And his insides went to mush. He was a jerk. Two days ago, he'd made her cry. "I'm sorry about the other day. I had no right to yell at you. You've never given me any reason to mistrust you"

"I'm sorry I accused you of trying to manipulate me."

Think you can work closely together with me crafting your designs?"

"I think so." She looked up at him. "I need to remember that all men aren't like my brother. Some are like my dad."

"Where do I fit in?"

Moonpie scrambled out of her arms, scampering to the food dish.

"You're a good man, Colson. I see that now. Your devotion to Cheyenne proves you're a man of character."

He searched the horizon. "My mom leaving us and the way Felicity was, it made me wary of women. You helped me realize there are good women in the world, but by the time I fell for you the first time I'd already bound myself to Felicity."

His gaze caught Resa's, stole her breath.

Fell for her the first time. Did that mean he'd fallen for her a second time?

"I'm sorry I left back then, without explaining why. Once I found out Felicity was pregnant, I had to go." Something in his eyes tugged at her. "I loved you so much. If I'd come back to explain, I'm not sure I'd have had the strength to walk away from you."

All moisture left her mouth, no words would form.

"Since Felicity's death, I've felt so guilty, I couldn't move on. But when I was in Kingsville, I saw Winston—the horse she'd been riding."

Her brain kicked into gear. "That must have been hard."

"Yes, but it was also freeing. A ten-year-old girl was riding him."

"Because you trained him properly."

"I get that now. And you've reminded me you're not like Felicity or my mom. I'm ready to move on now. With you. I never stopped loving you. Never forgot you."

A knot formed in her throat. "I never got over you. I tried, but you're the only man I've ever loved."

His mouth twitched, the corners tipped up. "Are you aware there's a sprig of mistletoe above us?"

She looked up. There it was, directly over their heads.

"I'd like to kiss you now. With no agenda. Well, maybe with just one. I'd like to kiss you because I love you and would like to spend the rest of my life with you ."

"I'd really like to kiss you, too. With the same agenda."

He cupped her cheek in his hand, dipped his head. His lips met hers.

Fireworks went off in her head and her heart. Her hands slid up his shoulders.

He ended the kiss, revealed the depth of his emotion with the intensity in his eyes. "I promise I'll stick around this time. Forever. I want to marry you—for you to be Cheyenne's mom."

"I like that plan." Tears blurred her vision. "So much. I already love her as if she were mine." She leaned her head against his shoulder as a contented sigh escaped. "You know, my ranch could use a good horse whisperer."

"I think I know somebody I could recommend." He kissed her again.

More fireworks.

"We should probably go back inside," he muttered against her lips. "Tell Cheyenne our news. She'll be so happy."

"Almost as happy as I am."

As six long years of separation melted away, this Christmas they had their own Texas holiday reunion to celebrate.

And a lifetime of love to share with the little girl who'd captured their hearts and drawn them back together.

* * * * *

If you loved Colson and Resa's story,
be sure to pick up the rest of the titles in the
TEXAS COWBOYS *series*

REUNITING WITH THE COWBOY
WINNING OVER THE COWBOY

Available now from Love Inspired!

Find more great reads at
www.LoveInspired.com

Dear Reader,

I've long loved reunion romances. Those stories of obstacles keeping the hero and heroine apart for years. Until finally, they work through their baggage and get to make up for all the time they lost.

Log furniture designer, beautiful heiress, Resa McCall had it all. But the man who completed her married someone else when the sins of his past caught up with him.

Almost six years after their whirlwind romance, with Resa in desperate need of a foreman, Colson came to her rescue. And Resa finally understood why he'd abandoned her.

But Colson had a secret eating him alive. Bandera was the last place he needed to be, the one place that could blow his world apart.

Colson and Resa had to rely on God and embrace the truth before they could stop being so stubborn and trust each other. These characters had long been in my head and I'm so glad they finally made it to paper.

I hope their story reflects my core belief—romance doesn't make the world go around—God does. Forever love is a blessing straight from Him.

Look for the final book in this series and discover why Devree, the wedding planner, is so pessimistic about taking the plunge.

Blessings,
Shannon Taylor Vannatter

Get 2 Free Books,
Plus 2 Free Gifts—
just for trying the Reader Service!